THE ROAD THROUGH MIDNIGHT

2/25/10

Dearest Isabel,

May you always have
God's brightest light for
your journey!

With love and
admiration,

Dotty

THE ROAD THROUGH MIDNIGHT

"Boomers" Caring for the
Greatest Generation

∞

Personal & Practical Insights for the Journey

Doretha Gurry

To order additional copies of this book, contact:
Xlibris Corporation
1-888-795-4274
www.Xlibris.com
Orders@Xlibris.com
57072

Contents

For my mother and father,

INTRODUCTION

JUST BEFORE THE Second World War my parents were married in a Catholic Church in Boston with Fr. Sullivan, the best man and a maid of honor as their only witnesses. Fifty years later their nine children gathered around a dining room table and decided to give them the wedding reception they never had. When the day came, we anxiously waited inside the country club ballroom until the whispers, "they're here" echoed and the room fell silent. Our eyes were fixed on the closed doors waiting for them to enter, anxious to see their expression. (This was to be the only time we *ever* pulled *anything* over on my mother.) They were escorted into the room to the music of "their song" and Mom was handed a silk bridal bouquet and Dad a boutonniere. Their party was complete. They shared their vows once more and this time had enough witnesses to fill a church. As a gift to them we planned a "*50th*" scrapbook. We had each taken pages home to be filled with our memories and photographs. I chose to write a poem that was not only a tribute to their love but also served as a brief history of their marriage. The poem, once read, will help to introduce my family. It was called, *A "Thank You" To the Y.* This was my page for their scrapbook and I read it to them at their wedding reception:

A "Thank You" To The Y

It happened at the Y
When Richard first saw Lorraine,
Across the room her blue eyes said,
"Yes, I'd like to dance."

From that night on,
Richard's fate was sealed.
Without a second thought,
She stole his heart and gave him hers,
And soon they tied the knot.

The couple now in wedded bliss
Living in New York,
Had no idea the world outside
Would hand them such a shock.

Somehow a war they never imagined
Figured in their plans.
But here it was
And off he went!
Now it was all in God's hands.

Peace did come and at long last.
Her husband was home to stay.
The war had spared him.
Together again,
They were determined to make a new start.

With Richard Jr., Doug and Detra,
It wouldn't be that long
'Til their little Brighton bungalow
Would have no room within . . .
For Doretha, Deborah, Rita, and Dayle,
Were their Faulkland Street additions.

"Rooms! More rooms," they cried,
And they drove out of the city.
In Hingham they found a house with 13,
A yard, ocean view . . . so pretty!

It was just heaven and so they moved in,
The country replacing the city.

Tom and Steve were the Hingham additions
To the couple whose count was last seven.
Now when setting the table

And counting the plates,
The number would come to eleven.

Their family thrived on the love they had
And shared so generously,
They even had a sweet little angel
Watching over all of them in heaven.

Twenty years have passed.
Their family now grown,
A need to move again.
Farewell to Hingham!
Their home on Paige Street
And sweet thoughts of the past,
Time to wrap memories
And take them.
It's time to move on.
Time's passed.

Norwell is new and so are the dreams
Of the couple with plans to retire.
Their love in tact,
Their hearts as one,
They're a couple we all admire!

So, thanks to the Y,
And that fateful night
When Richard first saw Lorraine.
Fifty years later
Their love is as strong,
And their feelings are still the same!

Their reception ended with their family circled around them while they danced to Ann Murray's song, "May I have this Dance for the Rest of My Life" . . .

Mom and dad would celebrate their anniversary every year for thirteen more years until death parted them on October 20, 2004. That Wednesday, late in the afternoon, my mother died.

Each one of their nine children experienced this road that we traveled in a unique way and now hold their memories in their hearts. Acknowledging and respecting each one of these stories, I write from *my* particular vantage point with personal memories and practical lessons learned along the way. As a welcome surprise, it has also served as a balm for healing.

It begins with *The Discovery* of Mom's Alzheimer's disease, and moves on to Mom and Dad leaving their home and adjusting to life in *Assisted Living* and eventually into long term *Nursing Care*, the *Dreaded Decision*. This *letting go* process, though extremely painful, can lend itself to a search of *who we are* when all of the material things that define us are gone, when everything we own belongs to someone else. It can also bring us face to face with what we really believe, our faith, and to imagine what happens after we die. Discussions never shared when life is young and we are healthy but can lead to a sense of peace. I share with you how my mother's Alzheimer's disease affected her life and that of her family and how we found helpful adaptations to aid and comfort her. One of the most exciting lessons was to discover how *connected* we all are. These last years have afforded me a view of life through a larger lens. I am now convinced that in some way, we touch everyone we meet and that everyone touches us in turn. I share the difference each one of us can make in a stranger's life when we see him/her as a part of the universal family. I share, as well, the new bonds of friendship that are made as residents in nursing care reach out to one another and find comfort and companionship. As a result of my journey, I believe that all of life is *Connected*. I also believe, if we have the confidence to ask God for the grace we need, we will find light at the end of the road even after the darkest of nights.

While they are on earth our parents stand in an imaginary doorway between this world and the next. When they depart we step forward and take their place. My mother has traveled the road through the darkness of midnight into the light that follows, and now *I* stand in the doorway in her place. With her compass to guide me, standing now as a wiser person for sharing the journey with her, I feel as prepared as one can be for the many surprises life will hold.

PROLOGUE

WHEN I WAS growing up in a coastal town, south of Boston, Sunday morning was a time of worship followed by dinner with the entire family. Stores for the most part were closed, local school sports took the day off, and very few people went to work. Sunday was family day. Thirty cents would buy a gallon of gas or a loaf of bread. The ageless Dick Clark was *truly* young, and I was protected from the subject of old age and dying. I'm a "Baby Boomer". To have grown up in this era, for me was a blessing, except for the occasional drill of scrambling under my school desk in the eighth grade. I wasn't sure at the time why this was done, but it had something to do with the Russians. Neighbors, teachers, and my local parish all supported the message I was receiving at home that I was loved. I also believed that my parents were going to live forever.

By the time I began my awareness of the aging process, I was approaching middle age, (though in my mind still seventeen), and my parents were in their late seventies. They were *still* going to live forever! Our parents, this "Greatest Generation", now occupying what they refer to as *rest homes* are closing out this era and as our parents leave us, they are teaching us how to say good-bye with courage and faith and how to travel through places we never thought we would visit.

My story is shared knowing that "Baby Boomers" are deep into this process. Now in our sixties, the emphasis is all about how to stay young. Did you know that sixty is the new forty? Who else but a "Boomer" could have come up with that? Once again, we manage to put off the idea of ever becoming old. T.V. advertising sells everything one would need to look young, since the goal is to live long. Many of my generation, over 65 years of age, are starting new careers or not retiring at all. All of the focus is on the magic of creams, exercise and, oh yes, medicine cabinets full of pharmaceuticals to help us feel young. It's probably a good idea that we don't talk too much about old age, sickness, disability and dying. There really isn't anything that can prepare you for the reality. But by accompanying our parents into their senior years, there is useful information to be gained about this realm of midnight, of growing old and *letting go*.

THE DISCOVERY

M Y MOTHER IS sitting in the kitchen and Dad is making breakfast. Dad's hair is now tight to his head, white now replacing the dark brown curls of his youth. Tall, big boned, and still very muscular, he is standing at the stove in his white, round-collared Hanes T-shirt XXL and wearing tan pants held up by wide suspenders. Brown hair may have given way to gray, but his handsome features are still strong, and his very large hands are gently cracking eggs for breakfast.

I placed the box of lemon Danish that I stopped to buy on the counter and took a seat at the round, white kitchen table. I thought, looking over to Dad at the stove, isn't that sweet! What I didn't know was Mom, sitting with her hands wrapped around a warm cup of coffee and watching him from her favorite white rocking chair, had forgotten *how* to make breakfast. Dad, a retired college professor and CPA, never spent time in the kitchen. From the beginning, the kitchen was my mother's domain. Mom would write up a food list, call in her order, and have it delivered by the local grocer. She would take great pains to be sure the quality of the meat or fish was just perfect. You could hear her on the phone saying, "I'll take 16 pork chops, and don't bother sending them, Louie, if they are not center cut."

She would go through the boxes as they were placed on the kitchen table, examining every item. She was an outstanding cook, an excellent baker, and took pride in preparing dinner for her large family every night. Dad sat at the head of the long green Formica table edged with 3 inches of ribbed aluminum. It looked like a picnic table for a giant; instead it was a custom table built for our giant family. We would come running into the kitchen from upstairs or outside and fill the two wooden benches with wrought iron legs that ran the length of the table. When dinner was served, Mom would sit in her chair opposite Dad. The two of them would make eye contact after making a visual head count. Of course, clean hands, no rollers in your hair, "Don't play with your food, don't chew with your mouth open, and please pass the bread," were the basic rules we all understood.

When I think back now to the morning of my visit, it was odd that Mom who baked so extraordinarily well until she was 80, was not cooking breakfast or even making coffee. I was satisfied to believe what I saw was Dad just enjoying retirement and treating Mom to a well-deserved *break*. After all, Mom had been cooking and baking for an army for over sixty years. What I did notice about her was a gradual change in her behavior. Unwarranted displays of anger, frustration, paranoid thoughts, and irritability were traits I recognize in hindsight but never understood to be signs of my mother descending into the darkness of a disease. Only in hindsight do I understand that Dad was trying desperately to cover – up Mom's disease.

Mom and Dad now lived in a suburban home with fewer rooms, but it had a large yard and a swimming pool. There was a patio with a pretty garden off the kitchen. Their bedroom was upstairs, a drawback that would later prove dangerous.

Mom was now always in bed, no one knew why; she was "Just tired". Dad was preparing her meals and going to the staircase, placing the tray on the step above, taking a step, and repeating this action until he reached the top. After double knee replacements years ago, his knees were failing again. This *one step at a time* method of getting the tray upstairs was his way of adapting. He would proudly place the tray before her. Then the insidious voice of dementia would either say, "You call that food?" or "Are you trying to poison me?" To my father's dismay, she would often toss the tray to the floor; this we later learned was classic Alzheimer's behavior.

It wasn't until signs of dehydration appeared that dad called on all of us to intervene. Because of this added medical development, he felt he could no longer continue as her caregiver even with the help of my sister and her family living next door. What Mom needed now was medical help.

My mother was only 4'11" tall. My father was 6'. Most of us inherited Dad's height. She was, however, the matriarch! She was the voice of the family, and she "ran the ship". At Dad's request we gathered in her bedroom and gently asked why she wasn't getting out of bed. She said, "I don't have to." The truth we would discover later. What we did know was that we needed to get her out of bed, downstairs, and to the doctor: three things she *refused* to do. We kept asking, she kept refusing, and we were at a standoff. After refusing an ambulance, (they were only for sick people), we gently sat her up on the side of the bed and asked her to stand. Screams of pain followed.

What was going on? Someone placed a small desk chair beside her bed and we asked her to sit in it. It is heartbreaking to look back on this memory now, these adult children, sons and daughters, wanting to help, listening to her scream in defiance at every turn. Her youngest son and a grandson each took a side of the chair and lifted her to the landing at the top of the stairs outside of her bedroom. She didn't hear her daughters reassuring her. She was so full of fear and rage; she grabbed each spindle of the banister as they carried her down, once so tightly the men (both former football players) nearly lost their balance. We were all summarily doomed to hell for doing such a cruel thing to our mother. We all froze. I can remember glancing to the foot of the stairs looking into Dad's sad dark eyes mirroring every emotion I was feeling. A final choice was given to her, "We either do this, Mom, or we call an ambulance."

In the middle of the stairs, there was *no* going back. In spite of facing eternal damnation, thinking now only of her safety, we finally gave ourselves permission to take control. It was the very first time!

With all due respect to health care workers, *Emergency* Room Care should really be called something else. After the last seven years, I have a few suggestions. After eight hours of wading through paperwork and questions to Mom, "Who is the President? Can you spell w-e-l-c-o-m-e *backwards?*"

After listening to numerous threats from the patient that she was going to get up and *walk* out, we finally saw a doctor! Now, one of the incredible things about my mother was her ability to make a statement and have it taken as the absolute truth. One nurse who came to know her described her as very credible. She gave answers to the doctors questions that we knew weren't true. "Are you having any pain?"

"No, I don't even know why they brought me here. I'm fine. I'm probably healthier than you are!"

Then the doctor looked at *us*, because I think he believed *her.* He asked her to get up and walk for him. It was painful to watch this elegant, distinguished woman try and fail. X-rays would later show that she had *no* cartilage in her left knee. She had been walking bone on bone for some time. There was one of our answers. This powerful little dynamo was now sitting in an emergency room bed not sure why she was there. We were standing there with our jaws open, waiting for someone to tell us what to do next! Until now, it was always her!

Mom returned home, but due to her advanced age and Alzheimer's, surgery was not an option. Dad and family continued to care for her. There was never any mention of moving. They would be "just fine" this was their home. Where else would they go?

This all changed the day my father blacked out while carrying a tray upstairs and fell backward. He hit his head against the slate floor. We discovered Dad was keeping a secret of his own. He was feeling light headed, short of breath and silently suffering from chest pain. This serious head injury would have killed most men his age. But one pacemaker later and some time to heal, he recovered and returned home. He had survived losing his father at age twelve; Dad was the oldest in a family of five. He had survived the Depression. He had survived serving on an aircraft carrier in the Pacific during the Second World War. With his strong Maine roots, an uncanny ability to adapt and always remembering his father's words, "You never quit," he had learned how to survive. This fall, though not fatal, was the beginning of the discussion that eventually led to the decision to sell their home.

ASSISTED LIVING

ASSISTED LIVING IS a style of living that can be a welcomed opportunity if we are cognizant of the personal and financial benefits and are capable of making the decision sooner rather than later. In reality, it is the most difficult decision to make because it is a decision to give up our home and most of our belongings, the work of a lifetime, and especially because we must surrender our independence. It is hard to look at our future needs when we are healthy and doing just fine in the present. As in a great number of cases, my parents waited too long. It took an event like my father's fall to force their decision.

Today, however, more and more "Boomers" are looking at this decision much earlier, and some are transferring the ownership of their homes and property to their adult children because if it becomes necessary to be placed in nursing care, one's financial holdings are factored in going back five years. Since these laws have come to light, we are able to make adjustments accordingly because we have the benefit of time. When my parents sold their home, all of the proceeds were used to support them, first in Assisted Living and then in Nursing Care until the money was gone. Dad was allowed to hold out burial expenses for himself and was able to give a one-time "gift" to family members up to $10,000. After the money ran out, (it didn't take long at $4,000 to $6,000 a month times two), the government assumed the financial responsibility for their Nursing Care with my father's teaching and Navy pensions turned over to the state. It is painful to hear him ask today at ninety, "Where did all my money go?"

We remind him of the wonderful home he was fortunate enough to give his wife and family and the blessings that were his for eighty-eight years. We remind him of his many achievements, his quiet generosity and the lesson in selflessness that we all learned from him. For Dad who stepped into the role of man *of the house* at age twelve, his initiation into financial responsibility arrived early, and he took it very seriously. So much letting go was happening now, and not only of his material belongings but also of his financial independence.

Most people wait too long to enjoy the social benefits of what Assisted Living can offer. It often takes a life-altering or life-threatening event to convince people that this step might be for them. In the medical field this time period between good health and nursing care is often called a "five-year window" of opportunity that unfortunately is often missed. In an Assisted Living apartment, while in good health but needing minor assistance, one can enjoy meals prepared and served in a pretty dining room, scheduled social events, small groups taking art classes or playing bridge, small gardens available to tend, libraries, and beautifully decorated common rooms or large living rooms.

A new alternative has arisen. Some families and friends have combined forces, sold their individual homes, pooled their profits, and built one large community home to accommodate their future needs. Now that's innovative! In every case, it is a tough decision to make. At the end of the day, my parents were five years too late.

When Dad recovered, he was forced to see that for their health and safety, there was no choice but to sell their home so we began the process of packing up sixty years of their memories. We rented a mammoth-sized dumpster that was delivered and placed in the driveway. Since there were never any instructions or wishes from my parents on how to do this, because this was *never* going to happen, we asked them what to do, and they gave us the general idea. We did our best to sort out what would fit into their two room Assisted Living apartment and were left with the daunting task of what to do with the rest. When we sifted through the mountains of items purged from the cellar and the attic, closets, and cabinets, it was overwhelming. I remember one particular afternoon upstairs in my parents' bedroom with my sister sorting Mom's clothes. I came out of the room and looked over the balcony down into the huge living room. This grand room had cathedral ceilings with large beams and a white marble fireplace that stretched from wall to wall. This elegant room which had seen so many happy occasions stood empty but for the pile in the center of it. This pile was the "throw out" pile and was slated for the dumpster.

We found one of the biggest surprises in the attic: Mom's light brown fur hat that matched her mink stole. The mink stole now sits in a living room in the form of a Teddy bear wearing Mom's monogrammed initials *DLJ* on the bottom of his feet. Christmas lights that bubble and two green velvet pixies were uncovered in years of dust that once graced a dining room wall in the form of sconces. Deciding what to throw away, give away, send with them, store, I wasn't prepared for all of the emotions. The sight of that dumpster now snow coning with their past treasures stays with me. Discarded were items that were purchased decades ago, I'm sure with great joy and excitement. Items that had now lost their value and were considered old and out of date or broken were labeled and tossed away. Never to be seen again. The symbolism was not lost on any of us.

We opened the door to the new apartment, and my mother hit the roof!

Other than the fact that this petite woman was sitting in a small "transport" wheelchair, nothing gave away her age or infirmity. One would look at her and see a well-groomed, beautifully dressed woman. Her face was the most striking thing about her; she had soft skin with barely a wrinkle and a natural peach blush on her cheeks. Her hair was sandy blonde teased into a classic smooth style. The roots of her true color (white-gray) were just beginning to peek through since she was not making her weekly trip to the beauty salon. Up to now, nothing superseded Mom getting her hair done. Her daughters can name every one of her hairdressers, and each one of them thought *they* were Mom's best friend. My mother's eyes were bright blue, small, almond shaped and smiled when she laughed. At this moment, however, her eyes were fixed on us. We stood together once again, not knowing what to do until she spoke.

"I hope you don't think I'm going in *there!*" We finally coaxed her into what would become her new living room with a promise that we would look for a "more suitable" place. We promised we would do better.

In two weeks time Mom made an astonishing adjustment. When she was in her bed, her mind told her she was still upstairs in her home, and Dad was at work. When she was in the other room, she thought they had bought a pretty little home, and she thought it was "just enough for them, wasn't it adorable?" It helped that her familiar and very special things surrounded her. It's a story in itself what we each determine to be our "very special" things. I can't help but wonder what mine will be. I wonder still what my two sons might determine for me.

For my parents, it was their king size bed, (minus the footboard and canopy), one bureau with a television on top, two tall Irish dolls, and another small bureau placed in the closet. For the second room, they took a small love seat, their first, a brown hand-carved rocking chair, a small oval French coffee table, Dad's blue leather chair, their entertainment center, large T.V., VCRs and a round table. They also chose a curio filled with Mom's collection of Royal Albert, Old Country Roses, and items of sentimental value: a white porcelain Madonna, a bridal doll, and a clock that chimed. Dad brought boxes of files that filled the coat closet. Their custom-built white oak kitchen and built-in hutch with stained glass pineapples was replaced with a kitchen *area*. A microwave, a blender, toaster, their black Braun coffee pot, and a mini-refrigerator would be their new kitchen. Six everyday plates, coffee mugs, and glasses were placed in the two cabinets over the small sink. The walls were all white, and the wall-to-wall rug was brown. We added lace curtains to soften the starkness and hung pictures on the walls to make it feel more like home. They were each given alert necklaces in the case of an emergency. Mom wouldn't wear hers, "That's ridiculous," and made fun of Dad if he did, so the alert necklaces ended up in a drawer.

Driving up to this new address I was both sad and relieved. Sad that their lives had been so abruptly condensed, sad that we had *all* lost our home, the gathering place of so many family occasions and celebrations, sad that the mother I knew was disappearing. Especially sad was the day my father met with the director of the facility in the living room and left all of us speechless when he said slowly, "So this is where I am going to live until I die?"

I was sad that I had space in my heart but no space in *my* apartment to care for them. I felt sadness and guilt, but I was relieved that they were together.

This highly rated facility was beautiful. It had a grand entrance where you checked in with a receptionist, a large open common space, lovely dining rooms, a lake view, and a garage with private parking space for their Cadillac. The sale of their home had afforded them all of this. Other than taking advantage of the lake view from their apartment window, Mom and Dad did not enjoy all of the benefits this life style could offer. Meals served in a dining room, the company of interesting people of similar age and background, social events, concerts in the large common room with the grand piano overlooking the lake, trips planned to local events, or new friendships were all passed up. Dad was trying desperately to keep Mom calm, still not fully understanding the nature of her disease. His choices were made with only her in mind. The nursing staff was very helpful to the family in supplying us the latest research and medical information on *Alzheimer's.* Here is where we started to understand what we could expect in the months ahead. I clearly remember staring at the word, *Alzheimer,* and focusing on how to spell the last name of the doctor who was responsible for bringing this disease to light. As time passed, I came to know it all too well. Today with Web MD and Internet sites, *www.Alzheimer'sAssociation.org* and links to more sites, we are able to keep abreast of the latest medications and, more importantly, all of the promising research.

Mom and Dad had adapted to their new life and certainly to a new life style. Unfortunately for Dad, his life would never be the same. Mom had refused to let anyone into the apartment except the family and that included housekeeping. She also refused to go to the dining room, so lunch and dinner were, (by special arrangement and added cost), brought to them. With Dad's macular degeneration and Mom's condition, food often fell unnoticed onto the floor. One day Mom spilled something onto the rug that Dad tried to clean up using – bleach. That, of course, left a white circle on the brown rug! Dad told me about this mishap over the phone and asked if I could come up with an idea to cover up his handy work since it was right in the center of the living room. I brought my acrylic paints with me, knelt down on the floor, and started to blend colors until I came up with, I must say, a perfect color match to the rug. I applied the paint to the white circle; Dad was relieved, while Mom watched this exercise with amusement. I also left a spray bottle of Resolve.

Now Dad was doing laundry, cleaning the apartment, and making breakfast. Added to this was the fact that Mom was still not walking well and not able to reach the bathroom. To solve this problem, Dad had placed a commode in the closet of the bedroom, and he would get out of bed throughout the night to help her.

Somehow, my parents found a rhythm to their day. We planned a schedule for visiting that stretched out over the week. We shared our working schedules and our days off and arranged it so that someone would be there just about every day.

It took a while for me to get used to visiting this new home, and it was never known what kind of visit I would have. Mom's moods behind closed doors could be very volatile. I arrived one day to find all of her jewelry on the floor, under the bed, just everywhere! Dad, looking defeated, was sitting in his blue leather chair staring into the bedroom looking at Mom sitting on the bed playing with the jewelry. He asked, "Do you think you could pick up all of this and take out the valuable pieces? I can't see for sure, but I know it is all mixed in together."

He was right. Real diamond earrings were mixed with costume, pearls, and rhinestones. I can only guess what happened that her jewelry ended up where it did. I separated out her valuable jewelry and gave it to Dad for safekeeping and placed all of the costume pieces that were left into categories of bracelets, earrings, necklaces, etc., and put them into clear zip-lock bags. This way mom could take them out and spread them all over her bed to look at them, as she would do for hours, sometimes just pairing up earrings and necklaces, and I can only guess again that somewhere in her long term memory, outfits and events were conjured up that also matched.

It was my good luck to have inherited Mom's talent for baking, and I enjoyed bringing homemade desserts every time I would visit, recipes learned years ago in Mom's kitchen. For as long as I can remember, mom would have something homemade on her counter. It gave her pleasure to watch her family enjoy it. They both *loved* their sweets and were always appreciative of my effort to bring something that smelled "yummy" and had the taste of home.

Sometimes I would wash Mom's hair or paint her fingernails while we visited. We would redecorate the curio, taking out each piece of china and replacing it on the shelf, even though I was aware that the previous sister had just done the same thing. Mom and I dressed her 24" tall Irish dolls, dressed in full Irish dance costumes, with her jewelry and combed their hair, making ponytails or braids for them. As long as Mom and Dad were mobile, we would take drives or what they referred to as "a ride around the block." They still loved a trip to see the ocean and going out to eat. It was usually a two-person operation, with Mom *and* Dad unsteady on their legs. It was a joy to be out, and for that brief time, we tried to pretend that life was normal. But no matter how lovely the day was, when the car turned into the unfamiliar driveway, my mother would fall silent and ask, "What are we doing here?"

No one will ever know what this self-imposed sacrifice was like for dad. But we did know, by the choices he made, how much he adored his wife, and this example of fidelity and selflessness was admired by all of his children.

THE FALL

T HE PHONE RANG, "Dad's at
Mass General!"

He had sustained a massive head trauma. During the night he got out of
bed to help Mom. While walking around the bed he fell and hit his head on the
bureau. We went into full family alert or, as Dad would say in his Navy style,
"All hands on deck." Phone calls were made making sure all nine were notified.
Some of us went up to Mass General, and others *covered* Mom. She was still in
their apartment; confused and angry that Dad wasn't home from work yet. The
news from the hospital was not promising. He was unconscious with a serious
brain injury that would require surgery.

The surgery saved his life, but now he was suffering from seizures, and still
not able to speak or eat. We all understood the importance of family members
being present when a loved one who is seriously ill is in the hospital. Thanks to
our large family, we made a substantial *presence*. More than once it was not only
a case of being there but also of giving voice to what we saw or to what Mom or
Dad needed. One of many examples was when we were told that Dad needed a
procedure to prevent clots from entering his lungs, not uncommon when one is
prone in bed for so long. It was scheduled, and my son and I who happened to
be there that day, accompanied him as they brought him down to the surgical
wing. When we finally arrived outside of the operating room of Mass General,
I was shocked to hear my dad mutter an almost inaudible but very definite, "No
P-r-o-c-e-d-u-re!" I turned to my son and said, "Did you hear that?"

He had heard the same thing. I asked to speak to his surgeon, told him
what we heard and asked him to please explain to Dad why he was having this

procedure and what it would mean if he didn't. In the meantime I asked my son to call my brother to let him know what had happened; this was too much of a responsibility to bear alone. I needed the troops. The surgeon approached Dad, who was lying on the gurney in what looked like a *holding* room waiting for surgery, bent down over him close to his face, and patiently explained it all. He also made sure he understood that without it, he could die. I looked to Dad holding my breath, hoping that he would agree. He looked at me and then to the doctor and gave him a nod in agreement. This is one of so many times that our family involvement meant the difference between life and death. After some time, he was transferred to The Spaulding Rehabilitation Hospital. This would turn out to be nine months of Hell for Dad. For my poor mother, this was the beginning of a nightmare. Mom was the matriarch but Dad was the rock. He was the one who took care of everything! He was the one who taught *us* that you *never* quit, that you don't lose until you stop trying. At one time or another, we had all heard him say he wished he had a *magic wand* to make all of us happy all the time. Now we wished we had one for him! He was a brain injury patient, and we had no idea if he would ever recover.

As we visited, putting on the yellow robes and washing our hands coming and going, we learned all about rehab for brain injuries. We learned how to thicken drinks and Dad learned a new way to drink, by placing his chin on his right shoulder when he swallowed. We understood on the weekend, *nothing happens*, that there are many doctors involved in serious cases, and sometime too many medications are given. On this particular day when several of us had gathered around Dad's bed for a visit, what we found shocked us!

Dad was hallucinating! He had closed his mouth to medications, and was refusing to eat. When he finally spoke, after we pleaded with him to open his mouth and tell us what was wrong, he told us we were terrible children for trying to kill our mother, and he was so angry with us he *wanted* to die.

Well, after we recovered from our astonishment, we looked at each other and thought, what do we do now? We asked to see the doctor on duty. It was a weekend, so we were not very optimistic, but a doctor did come into the room, and I can see her as if it were yesterday. She looked at Dad's chart and read aloud all of the medications he had been taking, reading them off one at a time. Then she saw that OxyContin had been added recently. She consulted with the team and OxyContin was immediately removed. Once out of his system, Dad's hallucinations disappeared, and we all breathed a sigh of relief. Most important again, was the significance of having *family on the floor*. This is the phrase we would hear aides and nurses say when they knew a patient's family was present.

One afternoon weeks later, my brother and I met, by chance, in Dad's room and while we watched Dad lying on the bed sleeping, we thought his breathing wasn't quite right. We called the nurse in, who said it could be pneumonia and that he should be taken to MGH for x-rays. I learned that afternoon that Pneumonia is often called "a friend" to the elderly because they see it as a painless way to die. We rode with Dad in the ambulance to Mass General and were so hasty in our departure we left our cars at Spaulding. Dad did have pneumonia and stayed for treatment. Luckily for us, another brother had arrived at Mass General when he heard about Dad and drove us back. If we had one thing going for us, it was strength in numbers. We often joked and called ourselves The Waltons, each one with a talent, each one filling a need. Dad recovered and was transferred back to Spaulding Rehabilitation.

It took half a dozen of their nine children and a temp agency to work out a schedule to cover what Dad had been doing alone. By now, between Mom and Dad, we were no strangers to hospitals, rehab centers and the confidential lounges set aside for families waiting for *serious* news. Dad had survived a great deal, but this would be *the fall* that would change all of our lives forever.

THE DREADED DECISION

W HEN ONE DECIDES to move into Assisted Living, he/she goes through a medical evaluation. There are certain criteria to be met. It is not Nursing Care but Assisted Care. There is a nurse on staff, and there are aides to help you with medications. But, and there is no gentle way to say this, you must be capable of performing "bathroom" duties on your own. Or as one nurse put it, "once we have to *put on the gloves*, it is another level of care." Without Dad as her roommate, it was clear Mom could not live in this apartment on her own.

There it was, the question no adult child wants to answer, "How *do* we care for Mom?" We dreaded this day! This difficult and heart breaking decision had to be made. It is a story unto itself how a family functions during times of stress and illness. We were a large and by its very nature, complicated family. Somehow, and probably for the very first time, since we had never been faced with a problem of this magnitude, we managed to stay focused. Somehow we knew it was vital to the outcome and future health of our entire family that every one of us would be included and our opinions respected. It was as if everything was on the line. This effort made a strong impact. I remember at one of our first gatherings walking out of the room in frustration. My brother, (a surprise), followed me out to the kitchen and urged me to come back saying we would not continue until I returned, that everyone needed to be heard. Honestly, I don't think we ever functioned better. Maybe it was the intensity of the task, or the shear shock of it all, but it came as a welcome surprise and I was grateful. Not to say this collaboration lasted forever, it didn't. But that is another story for another time. That day and for many months to follow we were not "the boys" or "the girls"; we were Mom and Dad's nine adult children, one unit, searching for answers. Our parents needed parents, and we knew the decisions we would arrive at, would greatly impact their lives. We were making tough decisions for the people we loved. Individually we struggled with the questions facing us. Could *I* care for Mom at my home? Is my home wheelchair accessible, could I make it so? Can I leave my job to do this? Am I a terrible person for *not* doing this? Would it be fair to my family? Am I physically able to care for her? I don't think it was easy for any of us, and it wasn't decided without soul searching and many conversations separately and all together. We talked with Mom's doctors and did further research into this disease named after Dr. Alzheimer. We all met for a final time and a decision was reached.

Dad had now been transferred from Spaulding Rehab into a long-term, skilled care nursing home, and we chose to move Mom to an Alzheimer's apartment on the same grounds. Now mom could easily go to visit Dad each day, and we would visit both of them.

The morning of the move arrived. We were to move Mom once again, now to live in an Alzheimer unit, a wing of an Assisted Living building. Even now when I recall this day it brings back feelings I would much rather forget. Mom, of course, had no idea why we were there other than to take her out. That morning we bathed and dressed Mom and I did her hair. She was so sweet and cooperative I felt like Judas. She had no idea she was moving from this little cocoon where she had learned how to live. As we arrived at her new "home", I was flushed with the tension of the scene that was bound to occur. Prior to our arrival, the sisters had furnished and decorated her room with a twin bed and linens of pale yellow and soft green. Her two Irish dolls were there along with her curio and all of the memories contained within, and her clothes. We placed her lace curtains on the two windows and furnished her bathroom with matching towels and accessories. Her rocking chair was there, a small T.V. and her Bose radio. But given the smaller size of her new room, the rest of their belongings from the apartment would have to be added to storage.

She *knew* the instant we entered the room! Her shoulders tightened and she became silent. She was so angry at first she didn't say anything at all. Her jaw was tight and her eyes were screaming! Finally, the silence was broken. "Don't think I don't know what you're doing. How could you do this to your mother?"

When her eyes met mine, I felt every bit of her resentment and had to leave the room. My brothers did their best to console her, usually that works in an Irish family, but even the brothers' *magic* wasn't successful. For all her confusion, she *knew* what was happening to her, and she let us know in no uncertain terms, that she didn't like it. If we weren't doomed to Hell before, we certainly were now!

Dad was slowly recovering from his injury to the amazement of his doctors. He was now transferred to the second floor in the Nursing Home. We learned it's better to be on the second floor than on the third; third floor is primarily for seriously ill patients. In addition, the second floor had a lovely formal dining room. He was now able to transfer into a wheelchair, and we were able to wheel him over to visit Mom in her new room. This was a huge improvement since they had needed a hydraulic lift to get him into bed when he had arrived months earlier. We had been bringing Mom over to visit him until then. The visits would usually go well, until it was time to go, and Mom wanted to know, "Why can't I just stay here?"

No explanation was accepted and by now no explanation would have been understood. It was sad for us to watch; it was heartbreaking for both of them!

There were also visits when I would arrive to see mom and want to take her out for the day. Her reaction was always, "No", followed by, "I'm not feeling up to it today. Let's just stay here."

It was too frightening for her to leave the room she was familiar with and venture outside to the unknown. Understanding this and being respectful of *why* she said "No", I would slowly push the chair towards the door while gently reassuring her it would be nice for her to go outside, to feel the sun on her face once outside, I convinced her also, since we're outside, why not go for a ride? It was a new experience to contradict my mother. I had to learn to give myself permission to take the lead, knowing once we were outside, she would say, "Oh, isn't this wonderful!" And she *always* did!

I remember two favorite outings in particular. The first was a fall day with blustery winds, the day we went to Castle Island after a stop at the drive-thru window at Dunkin Donuts for coffee and, of course, a sweet. As we passed the boathouse, we looked up and saw bright colored sails against the blue sky. We thought, isn't it too late for sailboats. When we got closer and pulled into a parking spot, we realized we had come upon windsurfers taking advantage of the great breezes blowing off the ocean. We were both so surprised to see the colorful sight of red, yellow, and aqua sails and thrilled to watch this sport that was new to both of us. We got comfortable, and I played a cassette of Noel Henry that we both enjoyed. We sat there in the car staring out at the scene and sipping our coffee. When a song came on that Mom especially loved, we began harmonizing, combining my soprano with her alto voice. When the song ended, she said,

"Oh, let's sing that one again."

It was a true joy and a moment I have frozen in time like a photograph in a scrapbook. For that moment Mom was just my Mom. We were in South Boston at Pleasure Bay watching windsurfers, and the rest of the world was far, far away.

We went to Montillio's Bakery on the ride home to get some "goodies" for her room. She loved to have something to offer company when they came to visit, (old habits die hard). I pulled up to her building, parked, took the transport chair out of my trunk and placed it by her car door. She sat in the chair holding the box of pastry and we were still invigorated by the joy of the day. A strong breeze was blowing our hair all out of place. We hurried into the building laughing at her holding onto the box so it wouldn't blow away. When we got to the secured door and I entered the code on the pad, she whispered upon entering and seeing the residents, "My word, look at them. They're all half dead." Realizing she had stopped filtering long ago, I let that go, and like naughty schoolgirls late for class, we hurried down the hall.

My second favorite outing was to the Christmas Place. Knowing how much my mother loved the holidays and enjoyed all of the decorating that surrounded them, (she used to begin right after Halloween), I thought why not; it should be wheelchair accessible, and it's all on one floor. So off we went, after ignoring the predictable, "Oh no, I'm not up to it today." When we arrived and she saw what was on the other side of the door, she was in Heaven. Sights and sounds of Christmas were everywhere: lights, candy canes, decorations, animated characters, a large train, and rows and rows of sparkling Christmas trees. Then suddenly while going down an aisle with shelves full of boxed angels, she put her foot out and stopped the chair. She had spotted an angel she just had to have. She pointed it out, and I took it down to give her a closer look. As I handed it to her, she grabbed it to herself and rocked her shoulders side to side with delight. This illuminated angel with its blue gown and soft white feathers was meant for her. When we returned, we found the perfect spot for her angel, plugged her in, and sat together admiring how she glowed. The only thing that shined brighter that afternoon was the glow of excitement coming from my mother's face.

This was a day I was happy to write in her Memory Journal. Her Memory Journal was a hard-covered book with empty pages each one of us would write in when we visited. We would mark the day and the date, recall the details of our time together, and sign our name. When she was alone she would pick it up and read it. It calmed her and reminded her that we *were* there, even though she was sure she hadn't seen anyone for weeks.

Unfortunately, Mom couldn't remember that her left leg wasn't able to hold her when she walked. She would get out of bed at night and start walking to the bathroom. Sadly for her, this could cause an injury and, unfortunately, it did. We lovingly called her our Phoenix, always rising! For example, on one occasion, I whispered in her ear what I *thought* was my final good-bye. Her bandaged head was wet with dark, sticky blood and her peach skin was gray and lifeless. She was unconscious lying on a gurney in the emergency room wrapped in white sheets that made her appear even whiter, in a room where everything around her was either silver or metal. I remember thinking, what an impersonal and public place to express such intimate and private words. That night they were transferring her to Mass General with this serious head injury, and I thought she couldn't possibly survive. At the hospital the next morning I found her *sitting up* in her bed, her knees drawn up, and one leg crossed over the other, bouncing her foot in the air. I was greeted with, "Where have you been? Thank *God* you're finally here to take me home," (each one of us received the same greeting) followed by, "Where is your father and why isn't *he* here?" She had no understanding of what had happened to her husband.

The last mishap in her apartment resulted in her being moved into the same building as Dad to recover, third floor, and after being evaluated this time, it was clear Mom would need skilled care as well. One of the next *letting go* lessons was occasioned by this move. My brother, who had power of attorney, took on the responsibility of all of the financial arrangements as he had done from the beginning and continued to do for this entire journey. Now an assortment of sisters was standing in the middle of Mom's apartment wondering what we could take from here to a Nursing Home. We knew from Dad's experience there would be very few things she would be able to bring. The third exercise in peeling away and letting go of the things we could not take with us had begun. I can remember holding up items one at a time and making two piles of "yes" and "no". Now, looking at a restricted space and with no need for furniture, there would be very few of her belongings that would accompany her. Her cozy room that still had the look of home would have to be dismantled. In the end it was her clothes, the two Irish dolls, her mink Teddy bear, the porcelain Madonna, two black and white photos; Dad's B.U. graduation picture, Mom's engagement photo, and a collage of their children's H.S. graduation photos. I couldn't help but wonder if the nurses who cared for her, ever looked at this group photo and wondered, nine children . . . ? This question hung in my head and lay heavy on my heart.

For my parents this was a road of twists and turns on a journey they could never have imagined, and which brought them once again to share the same address. My parents were both residents in a long term, skilled care, nursing facility.

Mom was eventually moved down to the second floor though in a separate room from Dad. They would spend the morning separately in their individual routines of the Nursing Home. At noon Dad would have lunch in the dining room, which looked like a small restaurant with linen tablecloths and seasonal decorations. Mom could go to the small room adjacent to the dining room, where residents who needed assistance ate their meals, but most often she had a lunch tray brought to her room. As soon as Dad's meal was over, he would leave the dining room and head towards the wing where his wife was to spend the rest of the day together in her room or in the sunroom, until Dad's nurse would come to collect him for supper; he was, after all, her *patient*. When he left, no matter how many hours they had spent together, Mom didn't want him to go and didn't understand why he had to leave.

Mom and Dad were in the same building, and I was happy they were finally together again. I was also ready to concede that they were *not* going to live forever.

THE NURSING HOME

I HAD NEVER seen the inside of a nursing home until we started looking at all of the possibilities. We were still functioning well as a *unit* and groups of us would meet and visit the facilities on our list. We discovered the quality of care can vary from A to Z and don't let an elegant lobby fool you. We learned early on that just because the entrance is grand, doesn't mean the care is. We had decided on a facility with the help of input from many sources; families who had been through this recently, doctors, state reports and with many unannounced visits. I must say from here on my parents' story is both sad and beautiful.

By now my father's condition was stable. He was in a wheel chair having never regained the strength in his trunk muscles to stand or walk except to make transfers with the aid of a walker. His pacemaker was managing his heart well. He was able to eat and drink again. His eyesight was nearly gone, but he continued to try to salvage what he could of his peripheral vision to get by. He had survived what the nurses called a serious insult to the brain and was in remarkable condition considering the injuries he had suffered. My mother was also in a wheelchair, (due to her left knee), with a diminishing appetite, growing confusion and loss of memory. She was comforted only when she was with Dad or family. The *sun downing*, an anxious behavior suffered by Alzheimer's patients that occurs in the late afternoon, was being treated with drugs. New drugs to aid her memory were added and an additional drug to suppress the need to go, thus limiting her urge to get out of bed and walk. They were also treating her high blood pressure and *bad nerves*.

Here they were, *our* parents, not someone else's parents, in a nursing home. It was *our* turn to travel this road with them, and we were looking straight into midnight. The courage and strength Dad exhibited was our beacon of light. He seemed to hold back the dark, and we followed him through it. He had learned how to ask for help and suffered innumerable invasions of personal privacy due to the very nature of his condition and yet always displayed such dignity. He welcomed the freedom to "paddle" his wheelchair down to his wife's room. In his chair, with his feet in a walking motion on the floor and his hands pushing the wheels forward, he had learned how to get where he needed to go. He would sit with her for hours on end, sometimes even napping at the same time with their hands clasped together across their wheelchairs. Such devotion! He displayed incredible courage as he adapted to what life had dealt him. Through it all, he expressed very few complaints.

I can remember one day visiting with sisters, when we got off the elevator, the nurses pointed to Mom's room and giggled. When we asked what the joke was, they said, "Well, your father is in your mother's room. He has closed the door, and when we went to check on them, they were in an embrace, *kissing*."

We looked at each other and just smiled. We also knocked before we opened the door! They were the talk of the floor.

There are some practical things to know about nursing home care. One has to decide at the outset whether or not you will use the laundry service. We were so emotionally unglued by now, not only by Dad's, but also by Mom's condition, that we were unaware that most of Mom's clothes were dry clean only. Her clothing, sweaters, slacks and blouses all required special care. Only when her cashmere sweater came back from the laundry now a fit for a small doll, did it dawn on us that this institutional laundry was meant for wash and wear clothes only. (Luckily for her, we had at least removed the detachable mink collar.) One can choose to take laundry home and return it, or have everything labeled with name and room number and stick to washables. As time went on, we also learned that slacks with elastic waistbands and tops that went over-the-head were easier to get off and on.

For her entire life my mother's wardrobe was of the utmost importance. We would routinely go through her clothes at the end of each season. We would carefully store in mothballs and cheesecloth all of her woolens after they were dry-cleaned. After all, a moth will eat a hole in clothing if it detects the slightest hint of a food stain. It was a blessing that Mom wasn't aware that all of her clothes were so plain now.

If Mom's clothes were elegant and high maintenance then it would only follow that her shoes were something special too. But now her feet seemed to be swollen all the time and appeared too large for her designer shoes. The nurses suggested that we take her to a shoe store and have her feet sized with the idea of purchasing what my mother would previously refer to as "old lady" shoes. Well, again with all the roles tossed into the air, it turned out to be my oldest brother and myself driving Mom to a women's shoe store. This was the scene: We pull up to the store and, of course, Mom does not want to get out of the car. It's a bright sunny day but she is *not* cooperating. Did I mention she was also spoiled? Since we cannot size her feet without her, I go into the store and look for the manager. I explain that my 88 – year-old mother is out in the car and is in desperate need of having her feet measured correctly and that she isn't *able* to come in, poor dear. He graciously agrees to come out to the car with his silver, oval shaped device to measure mom's feet. My brother sees us coming and hops out of the car to open mom's door and asks her to swing her legs out. Because the sun is shining in her eyes he gets an umbrella from the trunk to shield her face. Don't ask! The store manager places Mom's foot gently down on the measuring device that is sitting on the ground and says, "Do you think you could stand up for just a second?"

He comes up with a measurement that is one full size larger and a width wider than what Mom has been wearing and explains that when we get older, the bones in our feet are softer and our feet spread. Sizing up not only Mom's foot but also her condition, he recommended a soft leather tie shoe that Mom thought of as a sporty sneaker. My brother bought two pairs, black and tan, and we were all very happy, especially Mom's feet! Then she asked us if she could wear them home, and I couldn't help but think of *the countless times* she had bought *us* shoes and we asked *her* if we could wear our new shoes home. The salesman placed her old shoes in the box and she wore her new shoes home just like we did when we were kids. She was so pleased with the support and the comfort, to hear her on the ride back; you would have thought she had invented the shoe herself.

Over the next few months the ravages of Alzheimer's disease were more and more evident as my mother's condition deteriorated. One of the saddest moments was visiting in her room while an Irish CD was playing and watching her mumble through the words she used to know so well, songs we sang together from the time I was a little girl. But today when we sang, looking at each other, her mouth was moving but no words could be retrieved. I'm not sure how much she realized it, but *I* knew I had *lost her!*

Mom was now exhibiting one of the final stages of Alzheimer's, a total lack of interest in food. In spite of the fact that we had all read about this disease and thought we were informed, watching as our mother suffered its symptoms was nothing we could have prepared for. My oldest sister was asked to fill out the necessary forms that the staff required, (due to Dad's macular degeneration), and she had been named Mom's proxy when we thought Dad was not going to survive his earlier head trauma. The life/death questions, DNR or no DNR, (do not resuscitate), what – are – your – wishes – if . . . questions. I was beside my sister at the nurses' station. We stood there elbow to elbow, leaning on the counter, looking down at the white sheets of paper, knowing how critical every answer would be. These medical questions were hard to read with *our mother* in mind. She took them one at a time, carefully responding, as she knew our parents would want her to. Thankfully, years earlier, my parents had the conversation about end of life care and now my mother's wishes had become promises by father would keep, and to her oldest daughter, my mother had shared her wishes as well. Here she stood because that day had come.

Time went on and the question of a feeding tube came up and caused us division for the first time. Dad's fear was that Mom would pull this tube out causing herself injury and that it would be cruel to use extraordinary means to prolong her life. In his words, "It would be wrong to ask her to suffer from a disease she could never recover from."

But, even though he understood this and it was her doctor's recommendation to take this natural and gentle course, hearing rumblings of confusion from some of his children he knew what he had to do. He wanted all of us to understand and to be at peace with this decision before anything was final. He called a family meeting at the nursing home and asked Mom's doctor to talk to the family. We arrived in twos and threes until the conference room was full. The *unit* relinquished its role and Dad was clearly the father in charge, and we were listening as his adult children. Dad asked the doctor to explain what *all* of the options were, given this new development. We listened to his medical explanation and he finished with, "If this was my own mother, this is the course I would choose for her, this is the natural course to take."

He explained that the organs in our mother's eighty-nine year old body were shutting down on their own and that nothing could stop this from happening. That she had fought a brave battle throughout this disease and her bad nerves had only complicated that. He explained that Hospice could come in to care for her, that this new tier of nurses would be capable of keeping her comfortable, that she would not *feel* thirst or hunger, and that the medications would actually put her in a peaceful state. This is what my father understood, and now we all understood it, too.

HOSPICE CARE

THANK GOD FOR the angels who are called to this vocation. Now more and more hospice organizations are present to patients and families in nursing home settings as well as in private homes. They say gently the excruciating words that are so hard to hear.

We met the hospice team assigned to Mom in Dad's room before going to visit her. She was now resting in a semi-conscious state in a private room. The nurse explained to us what to expect over the next few days and that they were doing everything possible to keep her comfortable. The priest was called and families from out of state were making travel arrangements to come home. The nursing staff had set up a reclining lounge chair beside Mom's bed that made it possible for Dad to stay with her day and night. The dining room staff brought in a cart with coffee and checked in with us regularly to see if there was anything they could do for us.

There was a prayer I had made up when I was with Mom one night when she was anxious and not able to settle down to go to sleep. She watched me as I spoke, and when I finished, her shoulders would relax into her pillow, and she would close her eyes in a peaceful sigh. Tuesday morning, while sitting on the side of her bed with one of my sisters on the other side and Dad holding her hand, I prayed this prayer out loud not knowing if she could hear me: "Heavenly Father, Almighty and loving God, wrap me in your spirit, and protect me while I sleep, I ask you this in Jesus name, Amen."

The three of us watched in astonishment as my mother raised her arm up off the bed into the air and with a large sweeping motion touched her index finger to her forehead and made a perfect and distinct sign of the cross.

Early on Wednesday morning I was talking with my sister from New York, who had kept in close contact. She sensed it was time for her to be with Mom and said, "What do you think, should I come today?" I told her I would pick her up at the train.

We were nearly all gathered together, "the four boys" and "the five girls" all feeling a little bit like children. This painful and difficult experience is a life event one must live through; there are no words to express it.

Late Wednesday afternoon we were in Mom's room, and it was time for the nurses to tend to her. They asked us to step aside for a moment. They had explained about her breathing and the signs that would be present when her body would be letting go. Now the time in between breaths was longer and we were preparing ourselves. We stepped away from her bed and some of us were in the hall while some were still arriving. Dad was in the room facing the hall with his back to Mom, and I stood beside his chair looking out at the hall. From behind me I heard one of the nurses whisper to the other, "Call them in quickly . . ." They called out to Dad to hurry. He grabbed Mom's hand and stared at her with sad, intense confusion. I think he thought if he just kept looking at her, he could prolong her life and hold back death. I assured him that *she knew* he was there! The very thought of not being there for her at her moment of death, was something he could not bear and he actually started to scream at himself for leaving her side. Mom died peacefully with her husband and children around her. After a time, I don't know how long since there was no sense of time, we asked Dad to let go of her hand and to place it into the hand of God. We assured him that God would take her hand now, and she would be safe at home with Him. This spiritual image gave him the courage to let her go. It gave him the ability to accept the reality that she had died. Then I did the strangest thing. For the first time since I had focused so intensely on calming Dad at the actual moment of her death, I looked over at my mother and I tried to fix her hair and lift her chin to close her mouth. I was so frantic in this effort the aide actually handed me a brush and I stroked her hair as I had done so many times before. Now *I* had to recognize that she was gone, and I, too, had to let her go!

For the last five days we were like a simmering volcano waiting for the release of pressure that was bubbling under the surface. Our mother was dead; our father was sitting beside her, giving voice to gut wrenching moans of grief. I wondered how we would ever function as a family without our matriarch and would Dad ever be able to survive this loss? These concerns evoked the sensitivities and insecurities of our childhood. Factions of our unit were in danger of collapse. Too many of us, as it turned out, were used to the role of *leader*, and it was difficult to accept regressing back to the pecking order of our childhood as plans were being *announced.* The imaginary hierarchy was re-established. I don't know how to explain it other than to say that none of us knew *how* to behave, and we returned to what was familiar. Grief has no blueprint, and we all go through it differently. We were all simply *grieving!* Some events in life are lived only once and in that moment. There is no preparing for them. This was one of them.

Realizing this could be an unpleasant handicap to the task ahead of us, we made an effort to give space to those who needed it, respect each other's differences, and agreed that we should all be allowed to grieve in our own way. All this was done without a word spoken. I don't think we ever agreed to who the leader was; there were several. You could feel the energy it was taking, but now more than ever, we also knew we needed each other, and we needed to be able to function.

The focus had to be on Dad. We worked together with Dad and saw to Mom's wishes for a Funeral Mass in our hometown parish and made the additional funeral arrangements. Some of us met at the funeral home, others at the florist, and others were with dad. Those of us who were near the church met for supper at a familiar diner near the harbor. Feeling stunned by our loss it was a comfortable and familiar feeling to be together as we sat around the table, "the boys" and "the girls", which only proves what they say about the Irish, "quick to boil, but also quick to forgive." We sat there and asked questions that began with, "Do you remember?" Now on the roller coaster ride of grief, it was hard to believe that in this moment on that ride, we actually laughed.

Living through these last five days, I had been compelled to write a brief piece about my mother, my version of a eulogy. For some unknown reason, I needed to explain who my mother was, and how much her husband loved her. I thought I was writing it to share with my father, to console him in the days to come. Of course, I was writing it to ease *my* pain. When I shared it with my sisters, they asked if I would read it to the family on Friday night at the wake. What they really said was, "You have *got* to share this with the family."

I think it might have had something to do with giving the *sisters* a voice. I talked with the priest before the wake that night. I told him I would nod to him after the final prayer, if I felt I was able to read it, and if not, to continue with the final blessing. An unexpected strength came over me as he finished the prayer. He looked to me, and I gave him a sign that I was going to try. I came forward, and with a strong voice that came from the bottom of my heart, I stood in front of my mother's casket with my father on my right, looked out at their enormous family overflowing the capacity of the room, and read it out loud. I share it here, in my desire to share both of them with you.

1917-Dorothy Lorraine Kannaly Towle-2004

As we watched Mom descend into an unknown universe and observed the layers of her personality disappear, what remained was a whispered repetition of, "I love my babies," "I love you Bobey," and "Oh my God, Sweet Jesus."

"I Love My Babies"

As a woman she was proud to say, "There was never any question, I had all of the children God sent me." She had ten. One angel and the nine of us. With the multiple layers of her personality, we each knew a different Mom.

Apron Mom

One of these layers was our Apron Mom. Her kitchen counter full of pie plates and bowls, flour everywhere and mounds of apples on the kitchen table. She would sit and make one long ribbon of peel from each apple as we watched this magic take place from her tiny strong hands. To spend time alone with her was precious, conversations were easy and her unique sense of humor always entertaining. We were her full time job. She took great pride in the food she prepared, only the best, in how she dressed us, only the best. She trained her daughters and spoiled her sons and instilled in us her love of music. A true Irish Mother.

Elegant Mom

No one, but no one, could dress up like Elegant Mom. She lived in the perfect era, adorned hats with large brims, furs, high heels, long kid gloves, and her favorite-big jewelry! With all of this artfully assembled, the essence of femininity, and her chin slightly in the air, there she was, our Elegant Mom!

Hostess Mom

Whether it was Brighton, Hingham or Norwell, her home was the epicenter of the family. She set a spectacular table and enjoyed expressing her creativity decorating, and entertaining.

"I Love You Bobey"

Her second mantra, "I love you Bobey." It is interesting that Mom and Dad's pet names for one another, Boe and Bobey, were used interchangeably. Only with her Kannaly guard down, did we observe that Mom's love for Dad was equal to his epic love for her. We could hear it in her desperate need to know, "What should I do?" "I'm scared", and "Where is your father?"

The answers were found when Dad would enter her room and calm her fears by placing his large gentle hands on her face saying, "I'm right here Boe, now calm yourself down, I'm right here", and she would go off to sleep. This incredibly strong woman could not bear to be alone. For all of her attitudes, she was not whole or safe without her husband. It is only fitting that when Mom was taken from us, it was Dad's hand she was holding and Dad's voice she heard comforting her.

"Oh My God, Sweet Jesus"

Her third prayer was, "Oh my God, Sweet Jesus." In the end, with all of the stripping away that accompanies this inevitable journey, she loved here babies, her husband and her God. Her Heavenly Father has now wrapped her in His Spirit and taken her home. We smile to think, now that she has God's ear, just how that conversation might be going!"

Your babies and your husband will forever love you, too!

DOROTHY L. TOWLE

1917-2004

MOM'S FUNERAL MASS was beautiful in every detail. We gathered together as a family in the church we were raised in, and each of us took part in this prayerful and distinguished Irish, Catholic farewell. My brother's eulogy captured my mother's essence, and he shared with everyone her devotion to her husband and her nine children and what it meant for all us to return to the parish where over thirty years of our childhood memories of celebrating sacraments had taken place. The two Irish priests on the altar gave the final blessing at the conclusion of the mass and the cantor sang the "Irish Blessing", and we tried to comfort ourselves with the image of our mother "resting gently in the palm of His hand."

Attending funerals in the past and watching a grieving family enter into the church was always difficult, and my heart would go out to them. I had never lost anyone close to me until now. Today following the mass, *I* was in the recessional, and I would feel for the very first time what it *actually* felt like to have a broken heart. I looked over and made eye contact with my close friends and I remember thinking to myself, "My God, this is really happening, this is really *my* family leaving now, to bury *our* mother."

By the time I left the church and got into my son's car to drive to the grave, I had completely fallen apart. My daughter-in-law reached out and held my hand but I was inconsolable. All of the strength that I had summoned on

Friday night had just vanished. I stood at the graveside, and when the priest completed the service, my feet froze to the spot I was standing on. I could not move. I would not move. I wasn't ready to say good-bye. I needed more time with my mother for conversations we never had. This was my *darkest* moment; this was *my midnight!* My younger son was standing close beside me holding my left arm; then he took off his over coat, and I sensed the warmth and the weight of it as he placed it on my shoulders. Though I never actually saw him, I felt both of his arms as he supported me with my husband standing directly behind me. I was completely unaware of anything else until from the right my youngest sister appeared in front of me. Then I heard her speak to me and say softly, "It's O.K. You don't have to leave. You don't have to do anything you don't want to do".

She gave me the permission I needed to stay there for as long as I needed and said she would wait with me for as long as that took. I looked up at the light brown glossy casket and noticed how bare it looked, then at all of the roses that had been placed on the ground in front of it, and with the voice of a ten year old, asked her if I could place a rose on top of it. I pulled two peach roses from a bouquet, one for me and one for my sister, and together we placed them on top of Mom's casket and stood for a while until I was able to walk away.

The family was gathering at my brother's home but I was in no shape to go anywhere.

Before I knew what had happened, I looked up to discover my son had driven us to the old house on Paige Street, the house I grew up in, and we were parked in front of it at the beach. My older son knew me well enough to know that being by the ocean was something that might help to soothe my pain. He was right! After being there with my husband, son and daughter-in-law lovingly waiting in silence, for I don't know *how* long, the ocean had done its magic. Staring at the movement of the water had slowed my racing heart, and I told them I was ready to join the family.

It would be two and a half years until I found the insight I needed to begin the true repair of my heart.

MY DAWN

THE ONLY WAY to survive the loss of a loved one, become whole, and move on is to work through the five stages of grief that follow. The order isn't important, and it is possible that we may not experience every one of them. But it is important to our healing that we recognize them and do the hard work that our loss requires. It can take as long as five years to assimilate the loss of a loved one into our lives, understanding there is no timetable, and each one of us will do it differently. Our grief is as individual as our fingerprints.

For me, it was two and a half years after the death of my mother, while in conversation with a Carmelite Monk that I found the insight I needed to begin the healing process. This was my *light!*

I had attended the Boston Catholic Women's Conference that March. There was a full day planned with speakers, exhibits, and lunch, ending with the Cardinal celebrating Mass. I was there primarily to hear Immaculee Ilibagiza, author of *Left to Tell.* Her presentation was so compelling you could hear a pin drop in an auditorium of 4,000 women. Throughout the day, on the top floor of the Boston Convention/Exhibition Center, the sacrament of Reconciliation (for "Boomers", Confession or Penance) was being offered. It was never my plan to attend, it never entered my mind, but an inner voice that kept nudging me, the kind you can imagine on your shoulder kept saying, "It's been a while, you know it would *feel good* to go, Go!"

Now, the other little voice, usually wearing red, sitting on my other shoulder replied by saying, "Me go to confession? I don't think so. I don't know if I have regained enough *trust* to go; those painful issues of betrayal that wounded my soul are still lingering in my heart."

That any ordained man of God could harm the most innocent-God's children, was a breach of trust I had not reconciled. Not to mention, I wasn't looking forward to stating how long it had been since my *last* confession. Due to these very issues, it wasn't exactly a week ago, the way it was when we were kids. Still, this overwhelming need to speak with a priest persisted until I couldn't think of anything else! There was a break in the program, and I told one of the women from my group that I was going upstairs to confession. She said, "Oh, I think I'll come too."

When we arrived at the top of the escalator we discovered, (in order to accommodate the huge crowd), confessions were being heard in a large hall. Over thirty priests were seated in folding chairs in an otherwise empty room in four rows, a discreet distance apart. The hallway waiting to get into the room was overflowing with women cued up in three long lines, one at each of the three entries. My negative voice said, "Forget it, this will take *way* too long." The other voice said, "Stay put!"

I finally got to the head of my line, and the priest closest to me motioned me over. However, while I was waiting, knowing that I really needed this to turn out *well*, I asked God to direct me to a priest that would "hear" me and looked to the far right corner of the room where I saw a Carmelite Monk. I had chosen this monk out of all of the priests hearing confessions, and I wanted to wait for *him*! I told the woman next in line to take my turn; I was going to wait and pointed toward the corner. When the chair beside the monk became vacant, I headed over and sat down.

Perhaps I am exposing too much here, but I think it is important to understand my dubious state of mind as I approached. I sat down and made eye contact with the monk and respectfully but emphatically said, "I don't know if I should even *be* here."

I did not start with the customary, "Bless me father." Though a bit surprised, after observing the depth of the emotion behind the look on my face, he sat back in his chair, and with great patience, he heard me out on the issues that had caused such pain. We discussed them, he acknowledged them, he shed light on how I could heal myself, and see these church issues from another angle, with God's help. Then he also heard me out on the issues I suffered over the loss of my mother and the conversations I needed, but never had with her. When we were nearly finished, he invited me to close my eyes and to imagine God walking toward me – *with my mother*, and to imagine God "re-introducing" her to me, after being in His presence. The monk asked me, "What do *you need* to hear from *her*?"

This spiritual exercise continued, and it proved to be just what I needed. I entered into a conversation with my mother and heard in her voice the words I longed to hear. What became clear to me was something I had always known, and now I was able to believe it, and let it take root in my heart.

I thank the Holy Spirit for directing me to, "Stay put," and for guiding me to the Carmelite Monk who shed *light* on how I could unlock my heart and begin to heal. Now I am able to talk with my mother, pray to her, cry and laugh out loud with her!

The grace I received from this sacrament must have been radiating from my face. The monk smiled at me and said, "I wish I had a mirror to show you the difference in your face right now, compared to when you first sat down."

The church scandal, brought to light in 2002, had caused an internal, spiritual battle causing me to question the hierarchy's judgment, making it difficult to trust. But now, in an unusual turn of events, through *this* man of God, I finally found peace.

After what I thought was only a few minutes, I turned around to leave, and to my complete surprise, the hall was empty. The lines were gone, and we were the only two people left! So engrossed in emotional conversation, with my back to the hall, I had no sense of time, and my *confession* had turned into an hour and a half of *spiritual direction*. When I returned downstairs to my friends, they were just buzzing with the possibilities of, *what* could have taken *that long* to confess!

Every birthday, my parents would tell me the story about the day I was born, January 25, 1947, the day I *first* met my mother. The hospital had told my parents I was a "blue baby" and I was not expected to live. After hearing this from the doctor, my father came rushing into the hospital room where my mother was calmly singing to me. My father was stunned and thought, my God, she couldn't have heard the news yet. My mother had heard, but when they told *her,* she said, "You're wrong, this baby is perfect! There is absolutely *nothing* wrong with her!"

She had already nicknamed me their *bran muffin.* (I was their fourth child, but the first to be born with Dad's dark eyes and hair.) Her maternal instincts were correct, and as it turned out, the doctor came back to apologize to my parents, explaining that the hospital had made a terrible mistake! My parents enjoyed telling me this story, along with how I got my nickname *each* and *every* birthday. When they did, I always considered myself fortunate to have this unique and precious image of "meeting" my mother, and now I have one more.

ALL EYES ON DAD

URING THEIR DECADES-OLD love affair, and, like any love affair, it had its high and low roads; my parents had one another and us. They had no outside friends, so we were obviously concerned about Dad's reaction to his loss. Mom was his foremost reason for living. I can hear him saying the night my mother died, "I don't know *what* I'm going to do *without* your mother."

I put my hand on his shoulder and said, "I know, Dad."

He looked into my eyes and answered me, separating each word, as he spoke, "You – have-*no* – idea!"

These words stung, but he was right, I had no idea. I did know, we all knew, that it would be important to find something for Dad to focus on, some kind of project to occupy his time and most importantly his mind.

For years we had been trying to convince Dad, (for the future generations of our family), to share his extraordinary actions while serving in the Navy during WWII. Here was our chance. We gingerly approached the subject, since most veterans of this war didn't and don't share their experiences freely, and he was no exception. Since he couldn't see to write, we mentioned that we could hire a professional writer. Her name was Joan. She could come and tape him talking into her recorder. She would type up his oral story and print a hard copy for all of us to have. Now, when he thought this was something *he* could do for *us*, he started to listen. The project took on a life of its own. Before we knew it, Dad was asking for index cards, and I took notes as he organized his thoughts and stories in true professorial style. The cards were organized by topic and each card had a *buzzword* on the top of it along with a few sentences. When Joan arrived,

I would hand the card to her, she would say the buzzword and then ask dad about it, and he would take it from there! His memory was astonishing and, as it turned out, so was his story! After several weeks of preparing and recording, it was complete. Joan, because of Dad's remarkable work prior to her arrival, was able to transcribe his story almost verbatim, *My Story – A Personal History* as told by Richard R.Towle. His dedication page read,

To my wife Lorraine, my lifelong inspiration, and to my children, who continue to reinforce that inspiration.

After the movie "Saving Private Ryan" premiered, there was a surge of interest in the WWII War Memorial in Washington led by Tom Hanks and Senator Bob Dole. Television spots asked for financial support for the project, which had been authorized by Congress in 1993.

As a birthday present to my father, in September 1999, I had registered him in The Book of Remembrance at *his* Memorial in Washington, D.C., (Honoree ID 468334). The project gave Dad great pride as he tracked its progress from the architect's sketches, to the ground breaking and to (enlarged) photos of the construction underway. It is easy to visit this site: *www.WWIImemorial.org* and, if you have a family member who served during this war, you can follow the steps to register him/her. It's a great project for a family to get involved in. It can open up the conversation between generations, and it gives a child a true sense of history along with a deeper understanding of the role their grandparents or great grandparents played in it.

Five years later, with the Memorial nearing completion we directed Dad's attention to this project and he took a personal interest in it once again. With his television on CNN, he listened to the live broadcast of the Dedication Ceremony on Memorial Day 2004.

Four of us visited the Memorial that summer after it opened and returned with pictures and stories for Dad. Since he couldn't make the trip in person, we brought a photo of him wearing his Navy cap and sat it on a wall with the Pacific Tower in the background. It was in the Pacific that he received a purple heart, a Captain's Commendation and his ship; USS WASP CV-18, received 7 battle stars. Each of us wore sun visors that read, WWII USS WASP, and we gathered close around Dad's photo, and a stranger, intrigued by our story, offered to take the picture. *Dad was at his memorial!* After following the project with great interest from the groundbreaking to the dedication, now he had a first hand account from his children and a photo poster in his room.

WE ARE ALL CONNECTED

WHILE SITTING IN his wheelchair now eighty-nine years old, wearing what looked like a blue football helmet to protect his head, nearly blind, and as lonely as one man could be, my father asked me, "What possible reason do you think God could have for keeping me alive? What can *I* do?"

Though my heart broke hearing the question, I firmly answered, "Maybe you are meant to help someone else Dad, maybe someone here!"

There were several high functioning residents on Dad's floor, meaning they had their faculties, and could carry on a conversation and share companionship. Eventually, Dad started to reach out to some of them. He met a man while sitting in the hall after lunch. His wheelchair was beside Dad's and, after saying, "Hello", Dad found out he had just lost his wife as well. John was ninety, a gentleman like dad, loved music and had a beautiful singing voice. He and John became good friends. To watch this new friendship unfold, this unexpected companionship develop into a true bond with concern for one another is simply beautiful. It is an example of what life can be like when we are there for one another. I believe we are *all* connected, and it was always meant to be, that John's path would cross Dad's. When Dad is missing from the dinner table, John will "paddle" to Dad's doorway and ask, "Rich, are you O.K.?" and when John is among the missing, Dad will do the same. Instead of bringing *one* homemade dessert for Dad, now I carry an oval shaped basket *filled* with goodies to be shared with his posse, and he always asks, "Did John and Tom and Karol and Louise and Joe and Patty Quinn get one of these?" Dad felt in a way *he* was giving a gift to *them,* and it was a good feeling for him to enjoy again. It's a good thing I love to bake!

Dad also loves to personally distribute the hand knit Prayer Shawls that I bring from the knitting group at the church. He carefully determines who he thinks would really enjoy this gift of love and who needs the soft comfort it will bring, wanting the residents who have very few visitors or family to have one first. To feel the *gift of giving* again, which was such a big part of Dad, helped him to connect with his old self.

On Christmas Eve, he even asked one of the nurses to go into one of the resident's rooms that he knew had no family and to place a dancing Santa on her table, (anonymously). Of course, my sister had given this Santa to him the year before, so one could call this *re-gifting.* The next morning he waited anxiously to hear what the woman's reaction was to the surprise that he had arranged to leave in her room. This was *so* Dad, and it gave him such joy.

Louise, whose only son works out of the country, is also on Dad's floor. While I was visiting her one afternoon, I remember admiring the quilt on her bed. She said her daughter-in-law had made it. Two weeks later, Louise wheeled into Dad's room with a large UPS box on her lap and a big grin on her face. She had called her daughter-in-law in Colorado and asked her if she would mail her a quilt for me. It gave her such joy to see my expression when I opened the box, and she was so very happy to be giving *me* a gift. When almost everything else had been taken away from her, she had found something to give. I was meant to connect with Louise and she with me. Though some days I feel I empty myself when I visit; my heart is always full when I leave.

Years earlier as a young mother I had learned from next-door neighbors who were well along in years how very important the human touch was to the elderly. I had brought over some muffins and, as I left, I stopped to hug Bernadine and patted her on the arm. This tall, stately woman said, "I don't remember when I was hugged last. One would think old age was catchy. People are sometimes afraid to touch old people like me; I guess they think we're going to break. Thank you for the hug!" I have never forgotten her words, and we can never underestimate the powerful effect the human touch can have, especially on the elderly.

These residents have found one answer to the frequently asked question, "Why am I here?" They know when one of them has been taken to the hospital, when one of them is not eating, and they know the details of their past and each of their family members who come to visit them. They know they are there for one another. To help him remember our names, John's daughter typed up a list and taped it to the arm of his wheelchair. When he sees you coming you get the warmest personal greeting, and I always remember to hold his hand and kiss him on the top of his head.

Another benefit of *reaching out* was that Dad discovered many veterans who had served in WWII living on the same floor. These unassuming veterans share their stories and engage in many hours of conversation. Most often they end with, "It was tough, but I was just doing my job; we were all just doing our job."

This humble generation owns such a rich history. Down the hall from Dad, and to the right, Patty and Joe Quinn reside together, another love affair of over 60 years. Both ninety years old, Joe served in the Army, was at the Battle of the Bulge, and served under General Patton. His wife, Patty, was a portrait artist, and the four walls of their room are covered with exquisite oil paintings of Joe, her children, and of the Blessed Mother. This unassuming couple has made a home out of this little room, two hospital size beds, two end tables, and a windowsill. Patty proudly gives the tour, explaining every portrait as if it was for the very first time. Their love for one another, combined with Joe's sense of humor and Patty's smile, light up the floor when you see them coming, and when they see me coming, you would think it was Christmas. They are so grateful that someone would take the time to come into their room, to share something homemade and to *listen* to them for a while. I'm sure I was meant to cross their path and that they were meant to cross mine.

One night last month, as I was leaving, most of the residents, (almost all in wheelchairs), were waiting in the hall to go into the dining room. Joe raised his hand high into the air and waved when he saw me. He hollered across the hall to me, "Hey, Dotty, when are you coming back?"

That was the last image I have of him. He died later that week. When you ask Patty how she is doing, she says, "I miss my Joe so very much, and I believe he is in Paradise."

She is just so lost without him. Her son, daughter, staff and friends have surrounded her with love and attention to aid her in her grief. Just the other day she said she wished she could find something useful to do with her time. She is thinking about organizing an afternoon tea in the sunroom. There will be others who will connect with her beautiful smile, and on it goes.

Of all of the examples I have witnessed over the last few years of how *connected* we are, the most unanticipated and powerful one came as I was leaving the nursing home two weeks after my mother died. As I turned to enter the elevator, I passed by a large family that had gathered in the visiting room to the right. This room has a very large fish tank, a couch, two chairs, a coffee table, and two tall silk plants, one in each corner. We've actually nick named it the *fish room* and it serves as a gathering place for residents and visitors. I didn't think much about this scene, except to observe that this family had the same look on their faces that all of us had, in the very same room, two weeks earlier. I thought to myself as I entered the elevator and pushed the button, how sad the road was that they were about to travel. Only one other person was on the elevator with me, and I had seen him leave this family seconds before. He was a man in his late forties. He was tanned, good looking, wearing a raincoat with a travel bag by his side. He also wore a look of frustration and pain on his face. I can remember actually taking a moment to decide whether or not to engage in conversation with him. I looked over again and decided to say, "Hello", and by the time the elevator reached the lobby; he had poured out his story. His name was Tom, he was from Florida, his mother was dying, and he had taken a cab from Logan to be with his family. With their mother hours from death, the family had gathered to say good-bye and make arrangements for her funeral. The family, however, was divided between whether or not to bury their mother in her Catholic religion or in the Evangelical religion that some family members had recently joined, and he was returning to Florida after a heated argument with them. After I recovered from the coincidence that *I* had a younger brother his age, named Tom, living in Florida, (how strange is that?), I said most sincerely, "There are some things in life that can only be done once!" If he left now he might regret it forever.

By now we were standing downstairs in the lobby talking, and I offered to return with him to talk with his family and to try to help him explain his position. He said, "It's already so late. Are you sure you have the time?"

His reply told me that he never really *wanted* to leave. I explained that I had lost my mother recently, came from a large family myself, and understood how complicated it could be. As we entered the elevator again and pushed the button to return to the second floor, he explained more details about his family, and I shared my background with him. When we got off the elevator, his family saw him. They were surprised; they were also puzzled to see a stranger returning with him. Tom introduced me and explained our encounter on the elevator. He then asked them if they would be willing to listen to me, since I had come back with him to try to help. To my surprise, they were very open to the idea. I began by explaining my recent loss, and they were very compassionate. I told them, I too, had many brothers and sisters, and I understood how frustrating it could be when everyone is talking and no one is listening. Then I explained my position on the staff of a Catholic Parish as a Pastoral Associate and also the active role I played in an Interfaith Organization and that perhaps this combined experience might help to shed some light on this disagreement.

It was meant to be that of all of the people coming and going that night, *I* was meant to connect with *this* man, on that elevator that very moment, that very night! The family was at such an impasse; they welcomed the offer of a stranger to help facilitate. After a lengthy period of everyone *listening* while each one was given the opportunity to *be heard,* and a lengthy discussion on Baptism, and both faiths, they came to a decision. The wake would be an opportunity for the evangelical members to express their faith, and their mother would be buried after a Catholic mass the next day. We left the room together, and they invited me to come with them as they said good night to their mother. Honestly, it had already been a very long day, it was late, I was tired and I was not looking forward to the long ride home. But when I looked over and saw Tom now talking with his family, I disguised my fatigue and said, "I would be happy to."

This large family, so deep in grief, was united as they encircled their mother's bed. Looking at their mother, thinking about my own mother, I asked them if they would like to pray. They did, and I began the Hail Mary. As one family, with two faiths, we prayed for her, together! It's a tender moment that I will never forget! That room is two doors down from my Dad, and I often think about that family when I pass by.

EMOTIONAL RELOCATION

A S TO DAD . . . he has done it! He has adapted again! He has managed to emotionally relocate his beloved wife into the deepest part of his heart.

If one could imagine grief as a trunk, that is attached to you, large and heavy, that you are unable to pick it up and that it prevents you from moving, then, after doing the hard work of grief, that trunk becomes a small brief case. You can pick it up and travel out of the room. You can go anywhere, taking it with you, carrying the memory of your loved one everywhere you go, as you move on!

Dad is now living for his children and looking forward to the next family event, or as my mother used to say, "The next big thing." His focus and motivation is to stay healthy enough to attend our family Kris Kringle party. This is our family's thirty-seven year old tradition of celebrating Christmas with one of "the nine" hosting it. We each take a turn, oldest to youngest, then back to the oldest again. On that day, Dad's "gang" will gather around him and celebrate Christmas, and he will ask us once again, "Do you know what *my* favorite part of Kris Kringle was?" He will rush to tell us before we can answer, and say, "Your mother, surrounded by *all* of the children, singing "Happy Birthday" to Baby Jesus and blowing out the candles on the cake." This is one of *his* special memories, frozen forever in time, like a picture in *his* scrapbook.

NAVIGATING MIDNIGHT AGAIN

R ECENTLY WHEN VISITING Dad, our conversation turned to talk about heaven and he asked, "What do *you* think it's *really* all about?" I said I believed heaven was being in the presence of God, and that at the end of the day it all depends on *how well we love.* Then I told him I thought *he* would get a front row seat, given how well *he* had loved; his wife, his children, his God, and he smiled. Then he shared a dream he had when Mom came into his room and sat down on the side of his bed. She was so happy, and she looked so beautiful! But after visiting with him for a long while, she got up, smiled, and walked away. He explained that when he woke up from the dream, he was *so* upset she was gone; he was sad for the rest of the day. After listening to his dream, I reminded him that they would be *together again,* some day, in heaven. He looked at me, leaned forward and with a twinkle in his eye whispered, "*I can't wait!*"

With every step on this road through midnight, I have been acutely aware that I will be traveling this road again. Led out of the dark of my mother's death, I have been able to look forward. But now, my father, in the words of his nurses, is failing. Dad is on "a slide" and in need of "comfort and care". All of these words, this language of Hospice Care, are delivered in the most gentle way by caring nurses and staff where dad has lived for four years. These caregivers have come to know and love him. They marvel at his devotion to his wife, and have come to know our family as we have invited them into our lives. These same nurses accompanied us through the loss of our mother, assisted the family as our attentions turned to Dad, and three years later, celebrated with us when Dad turned ninety. They understand how the recent loss of his brother, Phil, has broken his already fragile heart and weakened his spirit.

The two brothers, 89 and 90 years old, Dad in Massachusetts and Phil in Maine, both in Nursing Care, would spend hours each night talking on the phone from their beds. They would talk endlessly and never repeat a story because they had so much catching up to do. The two of them shared so many childhood experiences. In 1929, they lost their father when they were only eleven and twelve. Their mother and her five children were offered a bedroom to share in their grandfather's home. Because of the cramped space, early in the spring, Dad and Phil pitched a tent in the back yard and made a wooden floor. This would serve as their bedroom until late fall. Dad learned at a very young age, during The Depression, the harsh realities of life and how to adapt to them. The two brothers were more like twins, both strong in body and mind, hard working; mischievous, always competing as to which one was the smartest. (Hard to do, since both got A's.) Though I think Dad conceded to Uncle Phil's language abilities over his.

One story that captures their boyhood bond is the story Dad shared recently when dictating his journal to Joan. The two young brothers were walking along the rocky coastline of a beach in Maine on a blustery fall day. The waves were very high, and they ventured out on to some large rocks for a closer look. Suddenly, a wave took Phil off of his feet, and Dad grabbed him by his coat collar to prevent him from being pulled out into the rough surf. On his knees now, hanging over the rock, Dad held on to his younger brother with all his might, as each wave came in and out, fighting against his grip as they did. He didn't know how much longer he could hold on, he just knew he couldn't let go! Because it was autumn, the beach was empty, and there was no help in sight. Suddenly a man appeared behind Dad. He had seen the dangerous position the two boys were in from a distance. The stranger reached over Dad, timed the rush of the next wave, pulled Phil out of the water and placed him on the rock. Both exhausted and wet, they thanked the man and hurried home while agreeing, of course, they wouldn't tell their mother what had happened! They didn't count on her finding their soaking wet clothes, and the rest you can imagine.

This is one of so many childhood memories they relived, in great detail, while talking on the phone. When Dad told his brother, he had finally shared his stories in a journal, one of the first things Phil asked him was, "Did you tell the story about the time you saved my life at the ocean?" Understated, brilliant, strong and generous, they were mirror reflections of one another.

Lately Dad has been spending more of his days in bed and recently his nurse, Kathleen, stood beside his bed with her hand on his shoulder and in an attempt to draw him out asked, "Richard, why do you think you are feeling so sluggish?"

After pausing to collect his thoughts he simply replied, "Well, my brother Phil died. He was very special to me, and I miss him."

Over the last few months Dad's throat muscles have weakened and swallowing clear liquids has become *dangerous*. To prevent further aspirating, his diet now consists of puréed food and thickened drinks. He is placing his chin down on his shoulder, once again, to assist in swallowing. Each visit seems to be met with new information. We listen, we take it in, and we adjust. I guess one could say *we* adapt. We too, have Maine roots and the apples haven't fallen far from the tree. Now instead of bringing homemade pastries, I am bringing squash custard and homemade applesauce, and everyone is bringing Egg Nog.

While visiting last Monday, I spent most of the day holding Dad's hand while he slept.

Sitting in the chair by his bed, I couldn't help but spend time on each of the photographs that cover his walls. These many pictures of Dad not only decorate his room, they tell the story of his life. Pictures of early adulthood, his college graduation, at middle age fishing with his sons, teaching a class at B.U. while pointing at the chalkboard, both his 50th and 60th wedding anniversary photos, and a Christmas photograph of over seventy people, five rows deep, and in the center, Mom and Dad; yes, our annual Kris Kringle party. It was 2001; it was my turn to host that year. The host's duties were to set the location, send the invitations, organize the "drawing", plan the food and hire the Santa. As I pause and stay a while with this picture, it holds a memory of a personal loss, and the sorrow returns.

Later, when Dad woke up from his nap, he looked at me and knew *who* I was, but then his eyes searched for something familiar to tell him *where* he was. He looked to his left and hanging on the wall, he saw what he was looking for; he saw what has become his *touchstone*. It is a large formal portrait of their 50th anniversary, and it hangs on the wall beside his bed, across from the double window in his private room. Mom and Dad are within a circle, in a square frame of gold. "Elegant mom" has her chin just slightly in the air, with beautiful blond hair and a gaze from her bright blue eyes that travels right out of the picture. Her black, scooped-neck dress is trimmed with small beads just along the neckline and she is holding a nosegay of cream and gold. Positioned close behind her is Dad, with his broad shoulders barely fitting in the frame, sparkling dark brown eyes, and a big smile. He is wearing a black suit, white shirt, and a dark silk tie with touches of gold. When Dad's searching eyes fell on *that* portrait, *he knew* where he was. When I leave after a visit and drive in front of the building, I slow down and look up from my car to locate his room, and I see them, framed by his window.

It was now mid day, a lunch tray was carried in, and the aide placed it in front of Dad. I indicated I would be staying to feed him. When I stood up and took the cover off of the dish, I saw three colors of pureed food, orange, green and white. It reminded me of the electric dish I used, when feeding my boys over three decades ago, when they were babies; three separate compartments, three colors. Our roles were reversed. My parents fed me, and now I was feeding my dad his lunch. I thickened some ginger ale and added *my homemade* applesauce for dessert.

The nurse said they were going to try to get Dad up the next day, using the hydraulic lift, and have him sit in his chair for an hour or so, that it would be helpful in fighting the pneumonia that was still lingering.

When I left the room for the nurse to change the I.V. and tend to Dad, I was leaning against the wall outside the door with my hands clasped low behind my back looking at the floor. My emotional gage was on empty. Then, uttering his first full sentence of the day, I heard Dad say to his nurse, "Isn't it wonderful to have a daughter like Dotty?" I exhaled an audible sigh.

The oldest of "the nine" remember a strict Dad, a dad who returned from WWII, and like most veterans of that era, he "stuffed down" the trauma of war. Today they call such trauma; posttraumatic stress, but sixty years ago, for the most part, veterans returned to their families and picked up where they left off, left alone with the nightmares that haunted them. We all knew the very serious professor and C.P.A. Everyone knew the dad who dedicated every weekend to his home and family. Saturdays he spent working around the house with his children, completing his famous list of things to be done. Sundays following Mass, it was family time and time for relaxation, summers out in the boat or in the back yard. Mom and Dad loved to drive up to Maine, (or as Dad would say, down to Maine), and it was always exciting to hear a spontaneous, "Who wants to go for a ride?" and an assortment of us would pile into the limo sized Chrysler with its pull down jump seats. Without exception, weekends were spent with his wife and family.

And now each of us has heard our *gentle* Dad say, "I love you", and we cherish these private moments. When we hear him speak this way, age becomes irrelevant; and we are back on Paige Street.

And now it is clear to me why I am writing this story at this time, as it flows into real time, another time of midnight, as I prepare to say good-bye to my father. This gift of expression has been a blessing from God that is helping me to absorb this painful loss.

December 22nd has arrived, the Saturday before Christmas, and my oldest brother, in taking his turn planning our Kris Kringle party, decided on hosting it at the same restaurant we all met at three months earlier when we celebrated Dad's 90th. His thinking was, if there was any possibility of Dad rallying and actually making it that day, this location was conveniently located next door to his building, and if not, *we* could go over to see him in small groups throughout the day.

Sadly, Dad's health did not improve. To the contrary, he went into a serious decline, and family members *did* go to visit him throughout the day in small groups to wish their father, grandfather and great grandfather well.

I was prepared for the call that came at 3:30 a.m. on December 23rd, telling us to come. I had gone by to see Dad on my way home after the party and could see physical changes, signs of what could come at any time. Before I left, in an attempt to get closer to him, I released the guardrail that separated us and rested my head on his shoulder. Though he was not responsive, I believed he could still hear me, and I told him, "We are all fine, Dad. We will take care of each other, you've done *enough,* you get an "A" in being a dad, an "A" in being a husband, and God is waiting for you. It's time for you to go dancing with Mommy." And I hugged him *good night!*

My fear had always been that Dad would die in the middle of the night, alone. After I hung up the phone, I threw on the clothes that were on a chair from the night before and running a toothbrush over my teeth, I said to my husband, "Hand me the keys, I'm driving!"

We all started to arrive in pretty much the same condition. The staff kept adding chairs to the room until they couldn't fit one more, and then they poured out into the hall. The residents were all still asleep. We called a priest and in the darkness of the early morning we prayed together and listened to him share words of comfort as he anointed Dad. Close to 9:00 a.m., recognizing the signs that were present, one by one we placed our hands on him, as we moved close beside him. We watched his breathing, counting the seconds in between breaths increase from three, to six, then seven and finally ten.

Then staring at his chest we realized there would be no more, we watched as his spirit left us, we watched as Our Heavenly Father, took our father home. One emotion rose up against another, fighting for space in my body, as I sat suspended in time.

Some time later, residents and staff members came into the room to give their condolences and to share how much Richard had meant to them, people Dad had *connected* with and they all shared in our grief.

Over the last few years we had seen our share of large clear bags, full of ones belongings, left by the door of an empty room, indicating the death of a resident. We knew Dad's room would be packed up later that day, and we wanted, I should say, we needed, to take his pictures off the wall and take care of his things *ourselves.* So, "the boys" and "the girls" worked together in this small space, each one focusing on this emotional task. Somehow holding his belongings seemed to extend his presence. Before we started, one of the brothers asked, "Did Dad have any wishes for his things?"

The answer was the same as it was when Mom died, "If you gave it to them, they wanted you to have it."

This decision took all of the guessing out of the question, and it worked very well. After so many moves, this would be the last time we would place Dad's belongings into large clear bags, and it was painful! Our hearts were breaking, and once in a while one of us had to stop and share the emotions of the object we were holding, like his clip board with each of our names with corresponding phone numbers written two inches high in black marker, his glasses, (not used for two years), his hand warmers, the black box that recorded information from his pacemaker through the telephone, and the blue helmet. Each item spoke to the tremendous effort he had made, at every turn, to make the best of what he had.

When I opened the closet and saw his light tan jacket, it was my turn. My mind went to all of the rides we took when he could transfer from his wheelchair into my car. Then to the walks we shared when I wheeled him down to the harbor or around the grounds of his building, and we would visit outside on the patio or at the gazebo. I saw him on the harbor side of Castle Island, flying a kite. That day, a stranger, enjoying the freedom of motion and wind, saw us approach and seeing Dad in his chair, bent down and handed Dad the string. He flew a kite he couldn't see, but smiled at the thought of it. I remembered how I had brought his jacket home to wash it, removed the food stains from the front and scrubbed the cuffs until they were clean again. How many times I had zipped up this jacket, the jacket I was now holding in my arms, and put the collar up around his neck to keep him warm. Outside he would wear his sunglasses and his dark blue, WWII USS WASP cap, which was often acknowledged by a salute from another veteran. He loved to feel the sun and the ocean breeze. He just loved being outside!

Though our senses were numb, we were trying to make sure we were not forgetting anyone or anything. Well, O.K., there was one brief flurry of emotional bullets that went flying. But when this outburst happened, the difference was, we stopped and communicated. It was agreed that *nine* siblings were grieving and old issues had to be tabled. Apologies were made and very quickly we returned to work. We focused on the next task on a long list, (that feels like a mental fire drill), that is part of the ritual of "letting go".

RICHARD R. TOWLE

1917-2007

KEEPING IN MIND that Dad wanted a simple funeral, we honored his pre-arranged wishes and made arrangements for the final details accordingly. When we finally found a florist that could accommodate us, (the day after Christmas), we ordered a large blanket of red roses with greens of boxwood and holly with ten white roses placed in the center, indicating the nine children and their angel, with DAD on red ribbon. An arrangement from his 28 grandchildren and 26 great-grandchildren was also ordered. In lieu of additional flowers, donations were to be given to Catholic Charities. Two large posters, created for his birthday celebration, told the ninety-year story of his life and were displayed at his wake. Beside the casket we placed the *touchstone* portrait of our Father and Mother.

By the time one reaches the age of ninety, they have usually outlived most of the people in their lives and attendance at their services is usually sparse. But Dad's "gang" had multiplied. We had friends and co-workers who came to express their sorrow at the loss of our dad or granddad. Then, an hour into the wake, a visitor arrived to pay an unexpected tribute. He was a former student in Dad's Accounting class in 1953, at Boston University. He saw Dad's name in the newspaper notices and when he realized this Towle was *his* Professor Towle, he was compelled to share with us, the significant impact this one professor had made in his life. This sixty-nine year old man, a retired principal, shared memories and stories from 1953 with the excitement of a seventeen year old, and his memories were so fresh we were all spellbound.

The next morning, we entered Saint Paul's Church. Dad's five daughters stopped to place the pall on his casket. Then, his *thirteen* grandsons, led by his youngest, a Marine in dress uniform, escorted their grandfather to the altar where five priests and a deacon waited to con-celebrate his funeral mass. We were comforted with the Liturgy of the Word and the Eucharist. When the mass ended, everyone present was asked to silently take Dad into the quiet of their hearts as they remembered him. This was our eulogy. It was an idea suggested by my oldest brother and embraced by all of us. When I closed *my* eyes, flashes of memories flooded my head. My mind stopped on a childhood memory during a family vacation. Dad and I were swimming in the *cold* ocean water at Old Orchard Beach in Maine. We had been in the water, body surfing for so long, when we got out, we had to walk on the beach until we could feel our legs, and we laughed at how red they were. Remembering this, *I smiled!*

After the final blessing, Dad's grandsons came forward and gathered at the altar. Once again thirteen men took their positions in front, beside and behind their grandfather as they escorted him from the church. I watched this awesome sight and my eyes fell on my two sons as they walked past me along with their cousins, boys who had grown up to be such tall men, whenever they gathered around me; I lovingly called them "my trees". They looked so somber and stood so proud as they walked beside their grandfather for the last time.

Though I had been comforted by the spirituality of the morning, I had been secretly dreading what I knew would occur when it ended, the *sight* of my father's casket *leaving* the church. Fortunately, this rectangular fence of men protected my eyes.

On Saturday, January 5, 2008, Dad's remains were joined with Mom's at St. Paul's Cemetery. "The dash" following RICHARD R. TOWLE 9/12/1917 – will be completed with the date 12/23/07 on their simple headstone. The stone has a small cross at the top and is dark gray granite, with white lines that swirl through it. The white lines remind me of small ocean waves at low tide, as they break gently on the beach with long spaces in between. When my brother and I chose it three years ago, I liked the idea of motion in the stone.

The Catholic priest prayed with us as we laid our father to rest, and he asked God to welcome him into His Eternal Light and to grant him Eternal Peace. Taps were played and when the American Flag was presented to his eldest son, along with words of gratitude on behalf of the President of the United States and a grateful nation, words of thank you for the service Dad had rendered to his country, our hearts swelled with pride for *our hero* of "The Greatest Generation".

The nine days between Dad's funeral mass and his burial had taken an emotional toll on all of us. They say the build up to such an event is often *more* painful than the event itself, and for the most part that is true. On *that* day, standing at my parents' grave, staring at the small box sitting on a green tarp that contained my father's ashes, I was quite strong. I stood composed, remembering to "stay pretty" for Mom, and trying to "be brave" for Dad. I was focused on the living memory of them and of what I thought they would have expected of me. For ninety years, Dad had fought the good fight, he had kept the faith, and now he had finished his race. I was at peace with the idea of my father being freed from the body that trapped him, was rejoicing in the image of him being received into the light of God, and being joined with his wife and all those he loved who had gone before him.

When the ceremony was completed there was a still, serene silence. The priest stood beside us in this moment, for a time, then interrupted the motionless scene by coming up to each one of us, wishing us God's blessing, and then he departed. I stood there for a while longer until family members, moving cautiously over the snowy ground, broke my concentration.

My brother offered his home, once more, for anyone who wanted to come by. When he came up to invite me, I thanked him and then told him I wanted to go to the local diner on the harbor, the same restaurant filled with childhood memories that some of us had gathered at three years ago. Those who were not traveling, going back to work, or on to other commitments, turned our reservation for six into one for thirteen. After grouping several small tables together to accommodate us, we were seated. We shared memories of Hingham and of our parents and then I offered a toast, "To Dad"! "Slainte"!

The next morning, however, the unpredictability of grief reared its head. I woke up to the harsh reality that follows, the reality that my dad was lost to this world, and I would *never* be seeing him again, and the pain of it left me sobbing!

To bear this loss, I will have to utilize *everything* I have learned about "letting go", complete this road through midnight, and journey to dawn, once more!

*   *   *

A ROADMAP TO DAWN

THERE IS NO way one can go *around* the grieving process and the emotions that accompany it: denial, anger, bargaining, depression and finally acceptance. In order to heal, one must live *through it!* There can also be secondary emotions or side effects of grief, both physiological, due to our weakened immune system, and psychological. Just when we think we might be losing our minds, or that we must be the only person to ever suffer these feelings, it helps to understand that all of these emotions, these manifestations of grief, are *natural.* We are fortunate that grief support groups and grief counselors are available. Expressing our emotions today is not only accepted, it is encouraged. We are *all* given permission to cry, yes, even men! There is a reason we feel better after a *good cry.* Not only do we release our bottled up emotions, our tears actually release unwanted chemicals from our system. When we "lean into our grief," (*The New Day Journal* by Mauryeen O'Brien, O.P.), and "tell our story", healing does come. It is also helpful to keep in mind the ancient belief that *love is stronger than death!*

An indication that we are searching for help on this journey is found in the popularity of a variety of books on the subject. So popular, they have made it to #1 on the "New York Times Bestseller List". These books offer us insight into this mystery of death.

For example, in 1992, Betty J. Eadie, wrote about her near death experience in the popular book, *Embraced by the Light.* Years later, another writer, Mitch Albom (author of *Tuesdays With Morrie*) wrote *The Five People You Meet In Heaven,* also a #1 bestseller.

Louise L. Hay is a world-renowned author, *Heal Your Body and You Can Heal Your Life,* and owns Hay House Publishing. Her simple message: "Every thought you think is creating your future", is powerful, and offers us a new way of using our minds to bring about health and healing.

Poets and writers, philosophers, and theologians all attempt to give us a glimpse into this realm of midnight and guide us to the light of dawn.

I believe, from my experience, if you have *one* good listener, a person who will *be present* to you, while you share the details of your loss, you are well on your way.

If you can consciously guide your spirit, to direct your mind, your body will heal and life *will* become gentle again, because *all* healing comes from within.

Science has finally caught up with the idea that our thoughts and our intentions can bring about healing. Dr. Wayne W. Dyer, *The Power of Intention*, and *Change Your Thoughts – Change Your Life*, is a pioneer in this field, and is a good example of one, who has for many years, offered the philosophy that our thoughts have tremendous power.

With the recent surge in the popularity of yoga, and the Mind Body Connection, "Boomers" everywhere are seeking to tap into this goldmine of a resource, as more light is being shed on the possibilities of using our spirit in tandem with our mind as a viable formula for healing.

Today, we are also fortunate to have the Internet, and the ability to click on to *www.Ask.com*, or a similar site, type in a question, and have more information than we could imagine, appear before us, as we GO in search of answers.

At the end of a Yoga practice, one sits on the floor with legs folded, and with their hands pressed together in prayer position close to their heart, they motion to one another, and say Namaste. This salutation is a thank you and also a wish. The intention is to share one's light and to honor the light we each possess inside of us. It is also believed that our light and every other light that make up our universe are one. What a beautiful image.

As we age, and mortality becomes a personal reality, it is common to begin the search of a deeper meaning to this thing called *life* and to ask, "Why am I here?" and to give ourselves a spiritual check up. Sometimes all of the material things that we gather over a lifetime, that make us feel good about ourselves, leave us wanting, and our spirit searches for something *more*.

There are so many roads to the ultimate source of inner peace. As I have found comfort in my Catholic faith, I invite you to take some time to delve into *your* faith, the origin of your beliefs, as a source of spiritual strength. I'm reminded of the old axiom, "The winds of God blow freely, it is up to *us* to raise the sail." Now could be a good time to "go sailing".

May God's love and the love of family and friends comfort you as you endeavor to find your dawn.

"Namaste"!

*   *   *

ACKNOWLEDGEMENT

FIRST, I MUST thank my son, Darren, for his tireless efforts in convincing me that *I* could tell a story that was *worth sharing.* For the many hours he spent as my sounding board as I grieved the loss of my parents and for understanding that this project was my path to healing.

I acknowledge with love my four brothers and four sisters. Though I chose not to develop their characters in my story and endeavored instead to place the reader in their position, I am very proud to say, "I am one of nine" and always grateful that I was born into this *oh so large* Irish family.

To my three "editors": my brother Richard, and my friends Julie and Martha, all retired English teachers who probably did not need *one more paper to correct,* Thank you!

AFTERWARD

A Year of Firsts

DAD DIED ON December 23, 2007. Christmas was a new experience without *our* "Father Christmas". That was the first of many *firsts* to follow.

January 25th, just one month after Christmas, I could only imagine my parents calling me early in the morning to sing their unique version of "Happy Birthday". For the first time, I would not hear the story about the day I was born, the details of the scare I gave both of them when the doctor told them I would not live. This first birthday without them, I was a little girl with a broken heart.

Just a few weeks after Dad's death, the family received an invitation from Dad's Nursing Home to come to their annual Ecumenical Memorial Service. This was a way of giving the staff and fellow residents an opportunity to *remember* residents who had died over the past year, to say goodbye to friends who had made that special *connection*. It was held in the common room on the third floor, the same room that we all gathered in to hear music when we would visit Dad. He would often say, "Do you have time to stay and go upstairs?"

That meant he wanted to listen to the piano and hear a *sing a long* that would include a guaranteed "Heart of my Heart" and a set of military songs including his favorite, "Anchors Away". I can close my eyes and see the room now, filled with wheelchairs and walkers and sleepy residents coming to life at the first note of the music, waving little American flags with all of the patriotism and energy they could muster.

But with my family's grief so raw, we were not sure we would be strong enough to return, emotionally. After several phone calls back and forth, some of us who lived locally decided to go. Returning to the Nursing Home took some strength and lots of exhales and audible sighs were heard as we walked together along the sidewalk toward the building until familiar scents met us as we entered the front door.

When we got off the elevator on the third floor, Dad's friend John was getting off of the adjacent elevator at the same time. Our eyes met and an emotional reunion took place. This beautiful man of 92 years, reached his arms straight up and cried out saying, "I can't believe you are here." He called out all of our names, names that were still listed on the arm of his wheelchair. Through his tears he said, "It's like seeing Richard again", " It's so good to see you!"

He had a tight grip of my hand and wouldn't let go for the longest time. He shared how very much he missed my Dad and cried through his words.

Staff members and other residents passed us on their way into the room and some came up to greet us with hugs and to tell us how much they missed Dad and our visits. Then the minister entered the room, which was so full we were standing in the back. I saw his face and remembered him at once. He was the minister who was counseling the family in crisis three years ago. Strangers that I *connected* with one night and memories of their emotional struggle, their brother Tom, from Florida, and our *chance* conversation on the elevator came to mind. The minister shook my hand and said, "I remember you!"

The service began, prayers were expressed in both song and words and when the list of names was read, we listened for the name we had come to hear – *Richard R. Towle*. We remembered our father along with residents who had become his friends and with the nurses who had given him such loving care.

Sometimes strange behaviors accompany us on this the *road to dawn*. I discovered that I was unable to bake. Now that was a surprise! I thoroughly enjoyed baking. I especially enjoyed all of the baking I had done for my parents, for Dad and his "posse". But following Dad's death, I stopped baking. Even the basket I used to deliver these "goodies" that usually sat on the counter, was put away and out of sight! This went on for a few months.

As is the nature of grief, just when you think you will feel a certain way for the rest of your life, and you "make friends" with that thought, things change! My mother's birthday was coming up. The day came and I woke up thinking how nice it would be to bake her favorite squash custard pie! There I was, head in the oven, adding the nutmeg to the top of the custard. I was not only baking, I was smiling at the smells and memories that this activity was "cooking" up.

The first dream I had of my mother after she died, came as a surprise. She was standing in the doorway of my father's room at the Nursing Home. She had one hand on the wall, and the other hand on her hip. She looked young and healthy, her blond hair styled and Estee Lauder makeup just right. She was dressed in a stylish skirt and sweater. In the dream she was smiling as she looked into the room at all of us. She didn't say anything in the dream, other than what I could read from the expression on her face, a playful grin that spoke volumes.

The first dream I had of my father was also unexpected. He also appeared young and healthy. He was dressed in his business suit and wingtip shoes and was standing in the doorway of one of the rooms in my home. He entered the room, also without speaking, and sat close beside me. When I woke up, I remembered this dream in great detail. I couldn't help but feel how reassuring it was to feel his shoulder touching mine as we sat side by side in silence. What a gift.

This gift of strength that my father leaves me is also visited on the next generation. As they endeavor to navigate the world they live in, he often comes to mind as an example of courage and fortitude.

Thanksgiving was celebrated this year with familiar traditions and families reunited in gatherings large and small across the country. This year at my table, however, it was the first Thanksgiving without my parents and memories of the past were very present. I looked across my table and remembered Dad sitting there in his wheelchair. Just two years ago he was with us for dinner. I saw him enjoying his meal, and becoming "angry" when he got full because that prevented him from trying just *one more dessert*. But I shouldn't have been surprised by the nostalgia of the day. This past year has been a year of firsts, some surprises and uninvited sadness. But all of this is the nature of a grieving heart and I remind myself that it will change.

One year has gone by since the death of my father. This will be the first Kris Kringle that we will gather to celebrate Christmas without my parents. Every year at this party, at some point in the day, my father would be so amazed at the size of his family (nearly 100 now) he would lean over to my mother and say, "Wow, look what *we* started!"

They will both be in our hearts this year as we celebrate Christmas and my mother's spirit will lead the children when it is time to sing "Happy Birthday" to Baby Jesus!

Get Published, Inc!
Thorofare, NJ 08086
02 February, 2010
BA2010033